# CHANGING THE SUBJECT

ellipsis

• • •

press

# CHANGING
## the SUBJECT

STORIES BY

STEPHEN-PAUL MARTIN

"Safety Somewhere Else" and "Cell" originally appeared, with different titles and in slightly different form, in *Fiction International*; "The Health of the Nation" and "Stopping" appeared in the *Western Humanities Review*; "Stopping" also appeared in *Big Bridge* and *Rougarou*; "Food" was originally published in *Harp & Altar*; "Food" has also appeared in the *&NOW Anthology* (best innovative writing 2004-2009, published by Lake Forest College Press, 2009) and in *The Harp & Altar Anthology*. "Safety Somewhere Else" (2008) and "The Health of the Nation" (2006) appeared in the Obscure Publications chapbook series.

Thanks to Corey Frost and Eugene Lim for their careful and perceptive editing attention. Thanks to Mel Freilicher and Harold Jaffe for reading and responding to earlier versions of these stories.

**ellipsis press**
www.ellipsispress.com
Jackson Heights, New York

Book design by Corey Frost.

# CHANGING THE SUBJECT

# SAFETY SOMEWHERE ELSE

The greatest mistake of all time took place thousands of years ago, when God let Noah's family survive the flood. God's plan was to start a new human race with a man he thought he could trust, but the limits of Noah's moral awareness were obvious right from the start. No sooner had God's rainbow vanished into the clouds than Noah was getting drunk and cursing his grandson, declaring that Canaan's descendants—one-third of the future human race—would be the lowest of slaves, a monstrous over-reaction that would have tragic consequences for countless generations of innocent people. Clearly, Noah wasn't the man God thought he was.

If God had been smart, only non-human animals would have been on the ark. The human race would not have survived and gone on to destroy and/or mistreat all other creatures. Instead, God made a point of encouraging human domination, assuring Noah that "the fear of you and the dread of you shall be upon every beast of the earth." Why was someone as crazy as Noah given such ominous power? Why were all the animals put in such a compromised position? Had the "beasts of the earth" really done anything wrong?

History has consistently shown how cruel our species can be to other animals, even those we've domesticated. We call dogs our best friends, but think of the horrible treatment they often receive. I've had dogs all my life, and I know they can be great companions. So when I think about the disgusting things that happen to them in research labs, I go out of my way to set things right, especially when the crime hits close to home. The most extreme example of this took place twenty-five years ago in New York, when my friend Karl was living with his dog, a beagle he called the Buddha, in a basement apartment a few blocks south of Canal Street.

Karl woke one night at half past one with a ruptured appendix. He almost didn't make it to the emergency room. Other complications developed after the surgery, and he had to stay in the hospital for a month. His next-door neighbor was willing to feed the Buddha, but Karl's problems went beyond immediate care for his dog. He had no health insurance. Whatever he had in the bank was needed to pay his medical bills, leaving him with nothing to pay his rent. He was already three months behind, and the landlord lost his patience. He called the Salvation Army and had Karl's furniture taken away. He put an ad in the paper and got a new tenant the following day. By the time Karl's neighbor got home from work that night, there was no dog to feed. The landlord had taken the Buddha to the dog pound, which kept him forty-eight hours, then gave him to a medical research lab.

If I'd been in New York at the time, I would have tried to help out. At the very least, I could have saved the Buddha from the lab. But I was on tour with Karl's two other close friends, Charlie and Stu. Our band was in Japan, then Germany and Sweden, places where the cutting-edge music we'd learned to play had caught on quite nicely, though in the States people thought we sounded like stray dogs howling at the moon. The tour was fun, especially off stage, and we came home eager to tell Karl about all the wild things we'd done and seen, only to find him hospitalized and homeless.

When Karl finally got out, each of us offered him a place to stay. But he wanted a place of his own, so we gave him money to rent a room at the YMCA. Then he went to the animal shelter to look for the Buddha.

The receptionist was all smiles and friendly phrases. She searched her records and told him that the dog had never been there. But Karl had an ex-girlfriend who worked at the shelter, and though he didn't really want to talk to her—she'd left him for another man six months before—he needed someone who knew how to get around the official cover-ups and denials. Two days later, she knew the truth. She tried to protect Karl's feelings, making up a story about a freak accident at the lab, but he'd heard her lie before and he knew how to make her tell the truth. She finally admitted that the Buddha's eyes had been surgically removed as part of an experiment. Then the doctor had put him to sleep.

When Karl came over that night he was more upset than I'd ever seen him. He'd taken the Buddha off the street as a puppy five years before, claiming that the dog had approached him as a messenger from the universe. I didn't believe in messages from the universe, but over time it was clear that the Buddha was making a positive difference. Karl was becoming a better person, more dependable and sensitive than he'd been before. The dog was the center of Karl's life. Lovers and friends had come and gone, but the Buddha was always waiting for him to come home from work at night, greeting him at the door with eager eyes, wagging his tail. They'd played in Battery Park each morning before the sun came up. They'd taken trips all over the nation when

Karl's van was still running. The thought of someone cutting out the Buddha's eyes filled Karl with hate. It filled me with hate. It filled Stu and Charlie with hate when we called and told them. We'd all known the Buddha for years. We'd cuddled and played with him many times. We agreed that we had to find the doctor from the lab and make him pay. And not just financially.

Working through Karl's ex-girlfriend the next day, we found out who the doctor was and where he lived in Forest Hills. We drove to his house at midnight in Stu's old Chevy Impala. We picked the back-door lock, ripped the doctor out of bed, ignored the confused cries of his wife beside him, slammed him against the wall and knocked him unconscious, took his glasses from the dresser and squashed them into the floorboards, grabbed his wallet from the nightstand, dragged him into the kitchen, shoved him down an old wooden staircase into the basement, tied him tightly to a rotting support beam, tied his wife and two young daughters to folding chairs we found beneath the staircase.

The daughters were dazed and terrified. Their mother tried to make it seem that things weren't as bad as they looked. She smiled at them and talked to us in a calm familiar voice. But Karl cut her off with what sounded like a prepared announcement: Please forgive us for waking you up. We're not common criminals. Our visit here tonight is scientific in nature. My colleagues and I are concerned with the problem of blindness, not just in human beings, but throughout the animal kingdom. Our investigations have convinced us that blindness in animals can only be addressed by working with human subjects. We need to study human eyes, and what would be more appropriate than to study the trained eyes of a great scientist, the very same eyes that have studied the eyes of so many helpless animals. Through countless experiments, the doctor here has established the importance—indeed, the necessity—of surgically removing the eyes of his experimental subjects. Tonight this same necessity will be applied to the doctor himself!

At first I laughed. I thought he was just pretending to be a mad doctor in a movie. But when he pulled a switchblade out of his pocket I started to panic. I thought what we'd already done was revenge enough, especially with the doctor looking so damaged and pathetic. But Karl looked vicious, out of control, and all my vindictive excitement was suddenly gone. I turned away from the doctor's bleeding face in the dirty basement light. I knew that the law would define what we'd done as a crime. No one would even ask about the crime we'd been avenging.

I told the wife and daughters what the doctor had done to the Buddha. The wife had no reaction at first, apparently familiar with her husband's research methods. But then she gave me a sympathetic look, figuring she'd better seem concerned. The little girls looked horrified and the younger one started crying, as if she could see that her father had done something wrong and had to be punished.

The wife took a deep breath and said: Look, he didn't know it was your dog. He didn't know it was anyone's dog. The lab gets dogs from the shelter all the time.

Karl said: It doesn't matter whose dog it was. What he did was murder. Research is one thing; violence is another. And now it's time to perform another experiment. Now it's time—

She said: It was just an animal. You can't kill a man for killing a dog.

Karl said: Why not? What makes people so special? That dog meant just as much to me as your husband does to you. And my dog didn't deserve what happened to him. He didn't hurt anyone. Your husband did.

I followed his logic perfectly. But I knew I couldn't let him take a knife to the doctor's eyes. I grabbed his arm and led him upstairs to the kitchen, sitting him down at the table.

I said: Listen man, we've got his wallet. Let's rough him up a bit more, maybe knock his teeth out, or break his nose if we haven't already, and—

Karl nearly shouted: The man has to pay with his eyes!

I said: But what if we end up killing him? If we get caught, we'll be looking at murder charges. And I don't think I can bring myself to cut the guy's eyes out right in front of those two little girls. They're innocent. His wife is innocent. Even if we take them upstairs and they don't have to watch, their lives will be ruined. Or no—what am I saying? We'll have to kill them too. They can identify us.

Karl said: We've already gone too far. We might as well go all the way.

We heard the doctor's groggy voice downstairs, then Stu's voice calling the doctor a killer, then the doctor sounding alarmed and angry, Charlie telling him to shut up, the doctor threatening Stu and Charlie with lawyers, Stu telling him to shut up, the sound of the doctor coughing and clearing his throat, the doctor threatening Stu and Charlie with lawyers again, a sound which must have been Stu or Charlie breaking the doctor's nose or knocking his teeth out, the doctor's wife and girls screaming and crying, the wife accusing my friends of being monsters, Charlie accusing her of being married to a monster.

Karl stared at the wooden tabletop. He raised the knife above his head and slammed it down as hard as he could. It stuck up from the wood like a knife in a chunk of cheese. He started talking quietly, indistinctly, to himself. I asked him what he was saying. He stared at the knife and got louder, speeding up and slowing down, as if the pace of his words had replaced their meaning. When I stood and tried to make him stop he just got louder and louder, speeding up and slowing down, gripping the sides of the table. His words were like a slaughterhouse of syllables, like pit bulls tearing each other apart in a billionaire's backyard, like wild applause in response to a bull collapsing with a sword in his back, or gunshots driving a herd of buffalo into a frenzy and over a cliff. He stopped, abruptly stood and looked through the window above the sink, as if his eyes were following the streetlights into the distance. I could tell that the crying of the girls downstairs was getting to him. After all, he had two baby sisters that he'd helped his aunt and uncle raise after his parents died. He shivered and yanked the knife out of the table, retracting the blade and putting it in his pocket. He looked outside again and the streetlights told him what to do next.

He went downstairs and said: Ladies, prepare yourself to watch a great artist in action. Stu, you still have your tattoo kit in your trunk, don't you? Go and get it.

Stu looked confused but nodded and went outside to get his equipment. When he wasn't making avant-garde music, Stu ran a mobile tattoo business out of his car, doing all his work in people's homes.

9

The wife took another deep breath and said: What are you doing?

Karl said: I'm making the punishment fit the crime. Your husband cut my dog's eyes *out of* his head. Now Stu is going to cut my dog's eyes *into* your husband's head.

She looked puzzled. Karl told her to wait and see. She struggled in her chair, cried out her husband's name. The doctor lifted his head, met her eyes briefly, passed out again. His face was a bloody mess.

When Stu returned with his toolbox, Karl said: Get ready, man. This is going to be your crowning achievement. You're going to give the doctor a new set of eyes. It's clear that he can't see things the way a dog sees them. So take your needle and cut the Buddha's eyes into the doctor's forehead, right above his eyebrows.

Stu looked like he wanted to laugh, but he saw that Karl wasn't joking.

The wife said: A tattoo?

Karl said: That's right, a tattoo. From now on, wherever the doctor goes, he'll see everything twice. Maybe then he'll *think* twice before he decides to cut animals up.

She said: That's totally sick! You're a fucking psycho!

Karl said: Actually, I'm not a fucking psycho. My friends here can tell you that I'm one of the nicest people in the world. I'm a good listener, and when one of my friends is in trouble I'll do anything to help him out. Sure, I lose my temper once in a while, but I've never hurt anyone before, at least not physically. But after what your husband did to my dog, he deserves—

She said: He was doing research. *Scientific* research! Can't you understand that? He was doing something for the good of the human race. He was trying to figure out how to make blind people see. He wasn't being sadistic.

Karl said: Normally you *ask* someone if it's okay before you start cutting them up. And I seriously doubt that your husband asked the Buddha to sign a consent form.

Red lights came flashing through the doorway at the top of the stairs. Apparently one of the neighbors, having heard all the screaming, had called the police. We made a quick exit, squeezing through a small basement window, got back to Stu's car through an alley and drove away undetected.

But we knew that we'd soon be in jail if we didn't make ourselves hard to find. Charlie came up with a plan, a way to vanish into the sea. He knew someone who knew someone who called himself Captain Green, a man who'd been in the Coast Guard in his twenties and early thirties, then got involved with Greenpeace as an anti-whaling activist. He'd used his connections to buy an old Coast Guard cutter for almost nothing, and now he spent most of his time hunting down whaling ships, ramming and sometimes sinking them or temporarily putting them out of commission. None of us had ever been at sea for more than a day. But Captain Green said he'd be glad to have us along, especially when we told him how much we respected the work he was doing.

We left from New York Harbor two days later. The ocean looked beautiful. But soon I was sure that we would have been more comfortable in jail. For the first two weeks we were seasick and dehydrated. Our beds were wooden bunks in a cramped compartment beside the engine room. The noise was so bad that for the first three nights we got no sleep. The latrine was out of commission. We had to piss and shit off the back of the ship, a difficult balancing act even when the deck wasn't pitching wildly. Often I found myself rehearsing a speech for Captain Green, begging him to take us home, though I figured he would just laugh and tell us to get tough and adjust. That's what we finally did, though only Karl really took to the sea.

At first I felt strange about ramming a ship. I knew that countless whales had been slaughtered over the years, and I thought that the captains of the whaling industry should be tried as mass murderers. But ramming and possibly sinking a ship seemed like a good way to get people killed. One of my crewmates told me that such things never happened. If a whaling ship was in danger of sinking, the captain sent out an SOS and help arrived in less than an hour, saving the crew, even if the ship itself went down. He also told me that whaling had been banned a few years before, that the ships we were hunting were in no position to take legal action against us. I nodded and smiled but still wasn't sure what to think—until we encountered a whaling ship off the southern coast of Iceland.

Karl and three of our crewmates had positioned themselves in rubber lifeboats between the whaling ship and a group of humpback whales. The harpoon gunners couldn't fire while our boats were in the way. But suddenly Karl's boat was lifted high in the air by a massive swell, and when the boat dipped into the trough, the gunners had a clear view and opened fire. Two harpoons hit a female whale. Her blood spurted out all over the waves. Her screams were shocking, unbearable. Until that point, I'd assumed that whales took harpoons in silence.

I wanted the other whales to dive and try to save their lives. But the mate of the bleeding whale had other ideas. He turned and swam full speed toward the whaling ship, toward certain death. And not just his own certain death: It looked like Karl was about to get crushed. His boat was directly between the whale and his target.

For a second I thought that someone would know what to do. A second later I knew that there was nothing anyone could do. But the whale knew what to do. He made it look easy, leaping out of the water and sailing gracefully over Karl's head, crashing back into the waves and surging on toward the whaling ship. The harpoon guns at point-blank range opened fire. The whale's blood filled the waves. His cries were even more painful than his mate's. I couldn't stand it. I wanted to sink every whaling ship in the world.

I thought of Moby Dick ramming and sinking the *Pequod*, dragging Captain Ahab to the bottom of the sea. But why hadn't Herman Melville described the screams of harpooned whales? He'd served on whaling ships and he must have heard those tragic sounds many times. Was it possible that he didn't care, or that he thought that the voices of whales were aesthetically unimportant? Though the book had always been one of my favorites, I suddenly wasn't so sure.

But I was quite sure that something had to be done. I didn't have long to wait. Captain Green was already turning the ship and gunning the engines. I still remember the feeling of picking up speed, then the moment of impact, the shock of getting knocked off my feet and almost off the ship, the sound of metal crunching against metal, our ship jolting into reverse, pausing briefly to gather up the lifeboats, then backing and turning and sailing away, having given the other whales a chance to escape. I never found out if the whaling ship went down. We were out of sight in less than fifteen minutes.

A half-hour later, I found Karl sitting on his bunk, staring at the wall.

I said: Karl, talk to me. You look all messed up.

He said: I'm not all messed up. I'm trying to fully take in what just happened.

I said: I practically shit in my pants, and I was just watching. You must have been going crazy with that whale coming at you.

He said: For a second it was like being in a world without names. For a second there was something in the sky, something that only made sense in a world without names. Then there was all that blood, those horrible sounds. The whale was coming and then he was six feet above me, and his eye seemed even closer, maybe because it was so big, almost the size of my head. But the most amazing thing was the look in his eye, like he knew we weren't his enemies, like he knew we were trying to help. I know it sounds crazy, but I know what I saw when I looked in his eye. It was like when I used to look in the Buddha's eyes, and I knew he cared about me, and I knew he cared that I cared about him. That's the feeling I got when I looked at that whale. And it wasn't like I'd been with him for years and he'd learned

15

to love the way I fed him and played with him. We'd never seen each other before.

I said: He even made sure that he didn't whack you with his tail when he came down. And he did this even though other members of our species had just killed his mate in cold blood.

Karl said: That's right—in cold blood.

A few days later, Karl announced that he'd found his true calling. He told Captain Green that he wanted to spend the rest of his life saving whales, that he didn't care how violent things got. In fact, he wanted violence if it meant saving innocent lives. When he tried to convince us to stay, I knew it was probably the right thing to do. But Charlie and Stu and I were too selfish. We had our music to return to, songs to write and concerts to give.

We also felt oppressed by the food situation. Captain Green didn't believe in eating red meat, but even if he'd been a hardcore burger junkie like we were, the ship's galley space was too limited to keep and cook much ground beef. We joked about the menu at first, but within a few weeks it was driving us crazy. There was no escape from canned vegetables and pasta. Though we knew it was wrong to eat animals, we'd all been hooked on red meat since we graduated from baby food.

Ironically, it was an animal rights group that made it safe to go home. An organization called Freedom from Slaughter heard about our case and spent hours investigating and exposing the violent procedures of the lab where the doctor worked. The situation was widely publicized, and the outrage against the doctor and his colleagues was so extreme that their lawyer advised them to drop the charges. When our boat returned to the city, we weren't criminals anymore.

I was pleasantly shocked. I hadn't expected anything but bullshit from the legal profession. But when I heard that the lab's lawyer had three black labs of his own, I wasn't quite so surprised. People with dogs know that their animals are amazing creatures, capable of things that human beings will never understand. Time spent with animals puts you in a different place—and in some ways a more valuable place—than time spent with people. Now that I've moved from New York to San Diego, a city that sets aside large amounts of public space for dogs, I've adopted two dogs from the animal shelter, a black lab mix and a golden lab mix, and I see every day how special their companionship can be. There's no need to talk. I can go for days without saying anything to my dogs. This would not be possible with people, who tend to be uncomfortable with silence when it lasts more than a few seconds.

The obvious objection here is that words help people connect with each other in complex, beautiful ways that go beyond the simple connections that are possible with animals. But let's test this assumption by consulting *The Odyssey*, a renowned example of what people can do with words. I don't think I'm alone in my belief that the most moving scene in Homer's epic occurs when Odysseus, returning to his palace disguised as a beggar, is recognized by Argus, his neglected and aging dog, who lifts his head, wags his tail, and dies from excitement. The dog alone can see through the hero's disguise. Everyone else is fooled, even Penelope, who cautiously questions her husband to make sure he's not an imposter. What does the dog know that Penelope doesn't know? Even though Argus was only a puppy when Odysseus departed twenty years before, somehow he can feel or smell his master's essence, something Penelope apparently can't recognize. She can only determine her husband's identity by testing him. His claim that he's Odysseus is not enough. She knows that words are often tools of deception. But even the goddess Athene cannot disguise Odysseus fully enough to avoid his dog's non-verbal understanding.

So why do we assume that human intelligence, constructed by language, is superior to the ways of knowing other animals practice? Why do we try to measure an animal's intelligence by comparing it to our own, running endless experiments, for example, to see if apes can be taught to speak? The obvious answer is that we can see only what our language tells us to see.

Other forms of perception are beyond our understanding. We can think about them only in the terms our language proposes, the pictures and mental designs our words create. These designs have helped us build the technologies we use to dominate the rest of the animal kingdom, leading us to develop our ongoing sense of superiority. But who can recall the smirking face of former President George W. Bush, for eight years in charge of the world's most powerful nation, without realizing how delusional our master species complex really is?

At times, I catch myself thinking that those who voted for Bush were sub-human idiots. But some Republicans are actually quite brilliant by mainstream standards and have even won Nobel Prizes for their research. An old friend of mine used to work for one of these brilliant people at a university here in San Diego. I discovered this only recently, when I ran into this friend—I'll call him Doug—at a café near the school. I like the café because it's on a hill and has views of the ocean in one direction and mountains in the other. It's also quiet. The owner is an ex-hippie who doesn't fill the place with media noise. Often I sit there for hours enjoying the scenery and reading.

When Doug walked in I didn't recognize him at first. I didn't even know he was in San Diego. I'd known him when we lived in New York, but we'd fallen out of touch, and the last time I'd seen him was more than twenty years ago, when he was a biology student at NYU. But he knew me right away and shook my hand eagerly. It turned out he'd been looking for a job without success and was getting desperate. I remembered him as being a brilliant, assertive person, so it surprised me that he was having trouble with his career.

When I asked him what the problem was, he looked around the room carefully, making sure that the wrong ears weren't listening. Then he said, or rather half-whispered: I know this is going to sound paranoid, but I'm getting screwed because I offended the wrong people.

I smiled: I've offended the wrong people many times myself, and I've paid the price, so you're talking to the right person.

He looked around the room quickly again before he said: Here's what happened. Maybe you heard that I got a post-doc here at the school?

I shook my head no.

He said: It was almost fifteen years ago. I thought I had it made. I'd hooked up with a neuro-biologist who'd almost gotten a Nobel Prize for his work on Alzheimer's. Initially I thought it was an honor to be working with him, and I'd been told that there might be an opening in his department, a full-time job. We got along so well that he was going to recommend me for the position. Everything seemed perfect. But after a while I couldn't stand what he was doing to the monkeys.

I made a face.

Doug said: I'd always told myself that we needed to use animals in medical research. I mean, without animal research we never would have come up with the polio vaccine and all sorts of other medical advances. But when I started working there and saw those monkeys in cages, it really got to me. I'd worked with rats and mice, and even with old dogs from the animal shelter. But this was different.

I made another face and said: My mother died of cancer. Some day scientists doing animal research might come up with a cure for cancer and AIDS and who knows what else. But I still can't stand the thought of taking animals and putting wires in their heads or strapping them down to an operating table. I remember in New York a friend of mine had a dog who ended up in a research lab, and—

Doug said: This neuroscientist didn't cut up any dogs while I was there, but he routinely put rhesus monkeys on the operating table. He'd slice open their flesh down to their skulls, then he'd drill his way through the bone to their brains and start poking around. I'm trained to deal with this kind of stuff. The first few times, I told myself not to let it bother me. I just went along with what was happening. But then there were times when I was in the lab by myself, since it was my job to give the monkeys their meals, and I'd go in and switch on this harsh overhead light in a room with a concrete floor and no vegetation of any kind and I'd see the monkeys looking at me from their cages. They were going crazy from boredom and isolation. The cages were way too small and each monkey was kept in a separate cage, with no other monkey to touch or play with, and monkeys don't do too well when they can't touch or play with each other, especially in sterile environments like this one.

I said: What bullshit! These people were scientists, right? They must have known what their monkeys needed. If you're planning to drill a hole in someone's skull, the least you can do is keep them comfortable before you torture them.

Doug said: I mentioned it to one of the other research assistants there, a guy who'd been there longer than I had, and he just laughed and said that the place was an animal *research* facility, not an animal *resort*. Anyway, one of these monkeys eventually chewed his own tail down to a bloody stump. Another one chewed his arm down to the bone. And then they'd end up on the operating table, and it would take the man hours to drill holes in their skulls, and the sound of that drill was way worse than any dentist drill I'd ever heard. After a while, I couldn't take it any more.

I said: So you quit?

Doug said: I didn't just quit. I also joined a local animal rights group. I wrote articles for their newsletter describing what was going on at the school. The articles got people upset. I'm surprised you didn't hear anything about it. I got lots of media—

I said: And now no one will give you a job?

He said: Now no one will give me a job. You don't rock the boat in this field. Getting a job is all about recommendations and connections, and I offended the wrong person. This guy knew everybody.

I said: There was no one outside his sphere of influence?

Doug said: Actually, there was, and I found a job with him for about six months, a guy named Larry Parker, who was trying to teach chimpanzees to talk, or at least use sign language. He was at a small college up in Oregon, and he treated his chimps like members of his family. They were in cages at night, but each one had at least one companion, and during the day they circulated freely in a large research compound filled with trees and other vegetation. Most of what Larry did with them involved games and observation. Nothing violent or invasive. I made sure of that before I agreed to work with him. I showed him the articles I'd written.

I said: I'm surprised that he wasn't afraid of hiring you.

Doug said: He was seen as an outsider anyway, and I think he figured that his grant money would keep coming in as long as he didn't do anything too extreme. At that point he wasn't active in the animal rights movement, though he told me that he liked what I'd written and he certainly felt that the animals he worked with had to be treated with respect. But a few months after I started working with him, he got a call from one of his colleagues who'd seen the way lab monkeys were being treated at the National Institutes of Health in Washington. So the next time Larry had business in the capital, he visited the D.C. labs himself and saw what his friend was talking about. He was totally disgusted. He came back with stories about how the NIH was driving their monkeys insane by keeping them in cages so small they could barely turn around, then killing them by drilling into their skulls or injecting them with deadly viruses. Pretty much the same thing I wrote about in my articles.

I said: But why did they let him visit the labs if they were doing these horrible things? Weren't they afraid of bad publicity?

Doug said: They didn't see anything wrong with it. They assumed they had nothing to hide. I think they figured that groups like PETA generally get regarded as a bunch of fanatics, especially when there's some kind of protest, and the people with the signs and megaphones appear on the news looking like raging hippies who forgot to get their Prozac prescriptions refilled. And like I told you before, everyone knows everyone else and you don't rock the boat, not with the National Institutes of Health. But after what he saw there, Larry stopped worrying about whose boat he might be rocking.

The waitress came and Doug ordered coffee. I ordered coffee and a spinach croissant and told Doug that the croissants were not to be missed, so he ordered one for himself, even though he said he was on a diet. Ever since the French had enraged right-wing Americans by opposing the U.S. war in Iraq, I'd been making a point in restaurants of ordering anything that sounded French.

Something caught the waitress's eye. I followed her gaze out the window, saw what she must have been looking at, but I couldn't say what it was. My eyes were prepared to tell me it was a cloud, but what I really saw was a globe of transparent glass filled with lightning bolts and rain, spinning slowly above the sea, maybe two miles distant. A second later it seemed to be less than a hundred yards away, even though it didn't look any larger. Then it disappeared, replaced by a line of pelicans gliding and dipping down and skimming the sea, rising and falling as each wave rose and fell. I looked back to see if the waitress was alarmed, but she'd already turned away to get our coffee and croissants. I thought of asking Doug if he'd seen what I had, but he wasn't facing the sea. He was watching the waitress.

I said: So Larry got more radical?

Doug turned back to face me with a lewd smile and said: Right. Larry got more radical, especially after he went to another research facility near Atlanta a few months later. They'd invited him there to give a talk on the progress he'd made in teaching his chimps to talk, and after his presentation he got taken on a tour of the facility, where he saw an adult male chimp in a five-by-five-by-seven-foot cage. I think Larry said they were calling him JoJo, or maybe it was Bozo or Bonzo—I can't remember—but I guess they figured if they gave him a name it would make their treatment of him sound more humane.

Doug looked across the room, where the waitress was nodding and smiling, taking the orders of a bloated couple with killer whales on matching Sea World t-shirts. He looked back at me and said: Anyway, JoJo had been there for ten years, with nothing in the cage but an old tire dangling at the end of a rope from the ceiling. That was supposed to be his source of amusement. Larry told me that all he had to do was look in JoJo's eyes and he could see that the chimp had been reduced to a state of terminal boredom and depression.

I shook my head and said: I remember when I

took my brother and his family to the San Diego Zoo, and the orangutans wouldn't even look in our direction. It was clear that they hated us. They didn't like being exhibits. But when I pointed this out to my brother, he just laughed and told me I was reading human emotions into animal behavior. He tried to tell me that animals don't have feelings. If he were here now, listening to what you're saying, he'd probably just claim that apes don't get bored and depressed, that only people feel those things.

Doug said: Then he'd have to be willfully deceiving himself. When JoJo saw that Larry was giving him a different kind of attention than he got from the lab personnel, he reached out between the bars of his cage to stroke Larry's face, and they held hands for a few minutes. Larry couldn't stop himself—he broke down and cried, even though there were other scientists there behaving like serious professionals, whatever that means. In that world keeping a straight face means being objective, so that people have to take you seriously.

I said: It's really that bad? I thought we were living in the age of the hip scientist who's actually a cool guy when you get past all the research and the terribly brilliant scientific papers he's published.

Doug said: That's just an image. When you get right down to it, these guys are all caught up in prestige and money, and that means taking yourself seriously when you're with colleagues. But Larry couldn't stop himself from crying. It really got to him—the sadness in JoJo's eyes, the tender way he was holding Larry's hand. He could never get the look in that chimp's eyes out of his mind. The whole experience got him so upset that he joined PETA and began writing articles and lobbying and picketing research facilities. And soon his government money stopped coming in, even though his work with the chimps has been recognized all over the world. So that was the end of my job. He couldn't afford an assistant any more.

I said: Sounds horrible. But how did Larry convince himself that his own work was okay? It sounds like he was still keeping his chimps in a restricted situation, even if he was being nice about it.

The waitress came back with our coffee and food, avoiding Doug's encouraging eyes and quickly turning away. For a second he looked like he might start crying. I remembered that back in New York I'd always felt strange about the contradictions in his behavior. On the one hand, he seemed like a sensitive, intelligent guy. On the other hand, he wasn't afraid to push his way to the front of the line, and he often went out of his way to use macho language. Any woman he wanted was a fox, and of course he himself was a wolf, not someone who spent all his time doing experiments and writing professional papers. But in the wake of the feminist movement, men with attitudes like his were seen by intelligent women as pigs, and I could see that he felt more unsure of himself than he had in the past, especially now that he couldn't find a job.

He shrugged and looked at his spinach croissant and said:  Actually, PETA wasn't too pleased when they came and saw that Larry kept the chimps in cages at night. But he told them that without some kind of research the human race would just go on treating animals like food or work machines and—

I said: But why did he want to teach chimps to talk? Why not just let them communicate in their own way?

Doug said: He wanted to show the world how smart they were.

I said: Talking equals smart?

Doug laughed: I can see you're not a scientist. What did you end up doing, by the way? Someone told me you were in law school after your career as a rock star ended.

I said: That lasted a year. I tried about ten other things after that, and now I'm a freelance photographer. Last week I was taking menu pictures, full-color shots of hamburgers and ham sandwiches, even though I don't eat meat anymore.

Laughter came from the next table. I turned to see myself looking back twice from the mirror shades of a white-haired woman wearing a big straw hat. She said: Do you really know what an animal is?

I glanced at Doug and we shared confused looks. Then I looked back at my doubled self in the woman's wraparound shades.

She said: A *real* animal, not a dog or a cat or some other cuddly, quasi-human creature. Have you ever actually met an animal in the wild?

I said: Where would I find the wild? Does it even exist anymore?

She smiled condescendingly and said: You have to know where to look.

I said: A former girlfriend once told me about a hiking trip she took in the Yukon wilderness, where she got cornered for several hours by a mountain lion. If a group of hikers hadn't come by and scared it away, the cat might have killed her. At the time, she was a hard-core member of the Animal Liberation Front. She'd spent time behind bars for letting animals out of their cages. But her feelings changed after that.

The woman said: My son was killed by a grizzly bear.

I didn't know what to say. I knew what I wanted to say, but I didn't want to create an unpleasant situation. I wanted to say that people kill people far more frequently than so-called wild animals do. I wanted to say that sharks, supposedly the most fearsome of all non-human creatures, are responsible for only two human deaths each year, whereas just in the U.S. more than two people had probably been killed by other people in the short time we'd been talking.

There was something unnerving about my face looking back at me twice from her shades. I could almost see the ocean behind my head in the depth of her lenses, dolphins leaping and splashing in the waves, the wall of mist in the place where the sky came down to meet the sea, a distance pulling me out of my body, forcing me to grip the sides of my chair, forcing me to penetrate the reflections in her glasses, penetrating her eyes and looking through her head and beyond, creating a tunnel of distance in the opposite direction, as if I were moving east against the motion of the sun, looking through the woman's face across the room and through French doors to a flagstone patio, where people in bright summer clothes were talking and laughing, while beyond them big white clouds floated over the desert floor, which ended eighty miles away where black peaks bit the sky and made it bleed, and sixty desert miles beyond those peaks was a government air force base, where planes had been designed in the form of huge translucent amoebas, energized by the sun to move at supersonic speeds, constantly changing their colors and shapes, piloted from the base by a tiny computer worth billions of dollars, planes that glowed in the dark and made people think they were looking at UFOs, and seventy miles northeast of the base was a UFO information center, a squat brick building filled with souvenirs and doctored photographs, open only one weekend a month, staffed by an elderly couple who'd been abducted fifteen years before, one of them convinced that they'd had a son before the abduction, the other convinced that they'd never had any children, that instead they'd been raising an orphaned chimpanzee before the abduction, and a hundred miles further east was the Grand Canyon, except that it wasn't there anymore, having been replaced by a hundred billion tourist pictures, images filling the canyon up to the rim, spilling out into parking lots and campsites, a garbage dump of burning clichés, replacing the sky with a fingerprint of smoke, making me feel unpleasantly hot as I looked back at myself in her wraparound shades.

She said: My son was *killed* by a grizzly bear.

I pulled my face away from the matching faces in her glasses. I said: What was your son like?

She kept staring at me. She lifted her upper lip with what looked like disdain. She said: What was my son *like*? How can you even think of asking me such a question? My son is dead. And you of all people should know *exactly* what my son was like. My son loved animals. He protested against the abuse of dogs and monkeys in research labs. He protested against oil companies drilling in wildlife habitats. And now he's dead, massacred by one of the animals he was trying to protect. I got to see his body—or what was left of it—when they brought it back from the Yukon. I'm sorry to say I didn't take any pictures, or I could show you what he looked like, though I guess that wouldn't *quite* be the same as telling you what he was *like*. What's *anyone* like? Is anyone like anyone else or anything else or—

I said: I guess not. I guess—

She said: Don't interrupt.

I felt embarrassed. I hate it when people interrupt me, and I pride myself on not interrupting others. In fact, I feel superior to most people simply because I don't interrupt them and most people I know interrupt me on a regular basis.

I told her I was sorry.

She said: I hate it when people interrupt me, and I pride myself on not interrupting other people. In fact, I feel superior to most people simply because I don't interrupt them and most people I know interrupt me on a regular basis.

I told her I was sorry.

She said: So don't interrupt me again, especially since I've got important things to tell you, things that should make you even more disgusted with our species than you already are, but maybe not as disgusted

33

as I was when I heard that my son had been arrested for breaking into a research lab, this place at Stanford where scientists were seeing what would happen if you took baby monkeys away from their mothers. Did they really need to spend millions of our tax dollars on experiments designed solely to figure out what should have been obvious even to a moron: that baby monkeys will be terrified, become depressed and probably go insane if you separate them from their mothers? How stupid can cruelty get? So my son and this group he was working with got arrested for breaking into the lab and liberating all the monkeys, making sure the poor creatures got sent back to the jungles where they belong. My son spent three years in jail for that. Can you believe it? Three years, for doing something that should have made him a hero.

She stopped talking but didn't turn her glasses away from my face. I couldn't stand the reflections any longer. I thought of changing the subject, a skill I've developed over the years because I don't like fighting with people. But I wanted to tell her the story of how three of my friends had also spent three years in jail, how they'd heard about a guy in northern Idaho making money running a bear-hunting farm, where he kept domesticated bears and offered people a chance to kill them on film, designer excitement for people willing to pay thousands of dollars to look like fearless hunters in the wild, except that the wild was carefully managed, populated by bears trained to be docile, even friendly, so friendly that when they saw people with guns, they walked up to them expecting to make friends, only to get their heads blown off by people who'd already paid for stuffed versions of the animals they would soon be killing. My friends had gotten so mad that they'd gone and released all the bears and then blown up the guy's house. I wanted to tell her this and other stories, but I couldn't face the awkward faces looking at me from her shades. I looked back at Doug hoping he would change the subject, and I wouldn't have to do it myself, since I hate it when people see that I'm afraid of confronting conflict. But he just sat there looking at me, trying hard to keep his face as blank as possible. He finally got up and shook my hand and said: Good seeing you. Let's keep in touch.

I watched him walk out the door knowing I'd probably never see him again. I thought briefly of all the other people I'd probably never see again, and their faces all became one face, a face I told myself I'd never seen before, until I realized it was mine. I ran my hands across my face just to make sure it was mine. Then I quickly looked around the room to make sure no one had seen what I was doing. All the other people in the café were touching their faces, looking around to make sure no one had seen what they were doing.

I thought of opening the book I'd been read-
ing, hoping the older woman would drop the conver-
sation. I knew if I turned and let my face get sucked
back into her glasses, I would no longer have any means
of preventing myself from becoming someone else, or
rather, becoming someone else twice, becoming her
son before and after his death. I tried to think of all the
reasons I couldn't be her son, the most obvious reason
being that she wasn't my mother, so I turned to her
planning to say that her son died for a good cause, and
how bicycle accidents kill more people each year than
grizzly bears have killed in the past hundred years. But
she was gone. The steam was still twisting up from her
ham and cheese omelet.

I sat there for the rest of the day, watching the
shadows of clouds gliding over the canyon, imagining
how different my life would have been if I'd been
raised by people destined in their old age to run a UFO
information center. Would I have grown up recalling
iridescent lights in the sky, a globe of rain with lightning
bolts, dogs barking incessantly for no apparent reason,
my parents disappearing for several hours, returning in
slightly modified form, unwilling or unable to talk about
where they'd been, convinced that they should adopt all
the orphaned chimpanzees in the world? Would I have
grown up assuming that every time my dogs barked
something strange or magical might happen? It's often

assumed that dogs have special abilities, a kind of ESP that alerts them to things that human beings can't detect, even with expensive technological devices.

Just an hour ago, for instance, my dogs began whimpering, pacing nervously around my living room. The phone rang. It was my cousin Frank. He and his family had just landed in San Diego and wanted to stop by for a few minutes before taking a vacation trip up the California coast. I generally try to avoid my cousin Frank. He's a Republican who likes to talk about his favorite primetime TV shows. We haven't seen each other in years, but soon he's at my door smiling and laughing, his wife is making herself at home at the kitchen table, and their two little boys are cowering in fear because they don't like dogs.

Trying to be a good host, I take the dogs into the backyard, assuming that if I smile and make small talk for a while, Cousin Frank and his family will decide to go to Sea World or the San Diego Zoo. But after I make a pot of coffee and put the boys in front of my computer, Cousin Frank starts criticizing President Obama for not being more aggressive in challenging Iran's nuclear-development program. Since I see no point in discussing politics with Republicans, I decide not to ask Cousin Frank why he thinks it's okay for the United States, a nation which still spends millions of dollars a day on hydrogen bombs, to respond with moral outrage when other countries even plan to make nuclear weapons. But his wife can sense that I think Cousin Frank's opinions are absurd, and before too long she decides that it's time to go to the zoo.

I'm relieved. But then Cousin Frank is urging me to come along, which I wouldn't do even if Cousin Frank were President of PETA. I can't stand zoos, even the supposedly humane San Diego Zoo. I can't stand looking at animals behind bars. They all look so trapped and depressed. The San Diego Zoo is famous for its animal habitats, designed to replicate the places where these animals might otherwise be living. This is nonsense. The so-called state-of-the-art enclosures and trails the zoo's reputation is based on are just disguised prisons, and the animals know it. After the time I went there with my brother, I swore I'd never go again, and I'm not about to break my vow. So I tell Cousin Frank that I've got an appointment to take photographs of grilled hot dogs in half an hour, and he can't really object because he didn't give me advance warning about their visit.

As soon as they leave, I take my dogs to the canyon. But after about thirty minutes dark clouds start to gather in the northern sky. The wind comes up, and soon it's raining. We're near a cave at the southern end of the canyon. My house is at the northern end, two miles away, so we scramble up into the cave and wait for the rain to stop. The view from the cave is usually outstanding. On relatively smog-free days, you can look south over the treetops and see the San Diego skyline, and beyond that the Coronado Bridge and the ocean.

But it keeps raining harder and harder, so hard that it's hard to see anything but rain. Soon there are flashes of lightning and the loudest thunderclaps I've ever heard. My dogs are terrified and cower in the back of the cave. I put their heads in my lap and try to help them feel safe, singing the songs I used to sing to them when they were puppies crying at night for their mothers. The rain shows no signs of letting up. It just keeps getting more intense. The gathering darkness feels like it might make all the light in the world obsolete. The sound of the rain in the trees is loud enough to make thinking obsolete.

Soon the dark has become opaque, solid and flat as a blackboard, and I'm sitting in a fifth grade classroom. The teacher is teaching us how to walk a dog, but the chalk in his hand keeps breaking. I want to tell him that before he tries to teach us how to walk dogs, he should learn how to write on a blackboard. But I'll get in trouble if I say something like that, and I've been in trouble many times before, to the point that a few weeks ago the principal called in my parents for a conference, advising them to send me to a special school for kids with behavior problems.

Now the teacher is drawing Noah's Ark on the blackboard, except that it's not a boat. It's a globe of rain with bolts of lightning. I raise my hand to complain, but no one else in the class looks worried, and the teacher ignores my hand and keeps on talking, explaining that Noah was chosen by God because he had magic powers, that before he was born people would plant wheat and get corn, or plant corn and get barley. But Noah's presence began to change everything. He was God's favorite person. God loved him so much that he gave him dominion over all non-human creatures, allowing them to survive only if they entered the Ark and became subject to human control.

The teacher's head gets hit by lightning, shattering and tumbling like an avalanche into the dark. Someone takes the teacher's place in the classroom, a man I've seen many times in the canyon, a guy in his early seventies with a lame Great Dane. He told me once that he got his dog from the animal shelter, that he'd rescued many dogs there over the years, and he always looked for the older ones that he figured no one else would want, since most people go to the shelter looking for puppies. But this man focused on dogs due to be put to sleep, or given away to research labs, figuring he could make their last few years as pleasant as possible, then go back and get another old dog and do the same thing. I remember leaving that conversation so moved that I went home with tears in my eyes, the same tears forming in my eyes right now as I realize that my dogs and I have been in the canyon all night, and the rain is still coming down, though it's not as opaque as before.

The gathering transparency is dreadful, slowly becoming a pane of glass so clear it can only shatter, breaking what it might have allowed me to see into sharp prismatic fragments. I want to put them carefully back together, building a rainbow, but everything is too sharp, as if the colors were forbidden, as if the mere act of giving them names would mean the end of all names. Instead, I try to give myself a new name, but I don't know what I should call myself, and suddenly I can't remember the name I already have.

Then a flash, a thunderclap. The rain abruptly stops. Something hovering over the canyon vanishes in the gathering light. I don't know what it was but something is making me say what it was: a globe of rain that came from the other side of time and space, collecting billions of animals, pairs of every species that the human race hasn't killed off yet, reducing them to microscopic versions of themselves, taking them all to a place that's free of predatory bipeds, restoring them to their normal size, commanding them to be fruitful and multiply and fill the earth, except of course that it's not the earth, and there won't be any dominant species turning it into the earth.

Suddenly the earth feels terribly small, terribly empty. I start to feel abandoned, but my dogs haven't left me behind. They're waking up, lifting their heads from my lap and sniffing the sunlight. The canyon is full of water almost up to the mouth of the cave, more than a hundred feet above the path where we take our walks. Looking south I see that the city is gone, completely submerged. There's nothing but surging water all the way to the place where the sky comes down.

# THE HEALTH OF THE NATION

Ten months ago, at a Zen retreat, I stared at a blank wall for seven days. The technical term for this strange behavior was meditation, and the ultimate goal was to break down the boundaries that separated me from the underlying unity of all things. But the lotus position was painful, and the pain kept getting worse. I felt no special connection to the universe, no underlying unity, except in the suffering I shared with the other people in the meditation hall. We sat motionless for hours, wishing we could get up and shake the tension out of our bodies, wondering why we were sitting there in a silence that only emphasized how banal and disturbing most of our thoughts and feelings were.

Actually, I knew why I was there. The reason had been bluntly summed up in the headline of a British newspaper in response to the November 2004 Presidential election: HOW CAN 59,054,087 PEOPLE BE SO STUPID? Like millions of non-conservative Americans, I was in shock in the weeks following the election, overwhelmed with disgust, embarrassed that I lived in such an aggressively mindless nation. At the same time, I didn't like the way I was wallowing in rage and contempt, hatching violent fantasies about punishing those who voted for Bush. I told myself that a more humane approach would be to view their ignorance with compassion. But was there room for compassion with a monster like Bush in the White House? Wasn't the nation badly in need of re-education camps? Shouldn't progressive people have been taking definite steps to secede from the union, or to move to a more intelligent part of the world? Angry questions like these wouldn't leave me alone, yet I wasn't prepared to do anything about them, and the impotence of my rage was getting painful. I needed something to clear my thinking. Though I'd been avoiding Zen for more than a year, I felt it was time to get back to the meditation cushion, so I called the teacher I'd been working with for the past five years and asked him to make a place for me in the Zen center's next retreat.

The term retreat is misleading. The Japanese word *sesshin* is closer to what really happens. I'm not sure what it literally means, but it refers to an induced crisis, a deliberate and concentrated assault on a person's normal state of awareness, a process similar in function to the initiation rituals shamans undergo in preparing themselves to become magicians and healers. I'd always been intimidated by the physical demands of sitting in the lotus position for hours on end. Even during my daily thirty-minute meditation sessions, I was in pain. But my teacher repeatedly insisted that true Zen progress could only be made in *sesshin*, and many Zen writers had echoed this opinion, so I was glad that I was finally ready to put myself to the test. I reminded myself that in the past I'd always learned something valuable from challenging situations. But as the days passed and I sat in pain on my cushion watching my thoughts keep cycling through the same frustrating patterns, I had to wonder if I hadn't been right in keeping Zen at a distance.

Still, the experience wasn't pointless. The silence I maintained throughout the *sesshin* gave me a new understanding of spoken communication. More than ever before, I saw how much mental energy is caught up in the process of talking, in our ongoing need to be prepared for whatever conversations come our way. As silence accumulated in my body over the seven days of the retreat, I understood why so many mystics become hermits, leaving the pressures of verbal interaction behind, releasing themselves from the need to perform in language, no longer trapped in the distorted mirrors people unavoidably hold up to each other. Since it was only my first retreat, I was still firmly trapped in my own distorted mirrors. Nor was I about to become a hermit. But I left the meditation hall with a strong desire to remain silent. So I got in my car and drove forty miles to the mountains east of San Diego, where after a strenuous climb I reached one of my favorite spots in the world, the summit of Garnet Peak.

I sat on a folded blanket resting my back on a smooth rock. North and south there were mountains as far as I could see. Behind me the sun was going down. At my feet was a cliff, a sheer drop of six thousand feet, looking out on a desert that ran east for thirty miles to a shallow inland sea, backdropped by another range of mountains. An unassuming silence rose from the desert into my body. Perhaps because of the hours I'd spent on my meditation cushion, the words that normally would have been narrating the passage of time faded into the twilight, and I was left with no thoughts or feelings about myself or anything else, no response to the vanishing landscape or the stars coming out above the mountains. At some point I began to get cold, so I wrapped myself in my blanket. I remember how nice it felt to get warm. Then the eastern sky began paling ever so slightly, the vague silhouettes of the mountains became more distinct, and I knew that the sun would soon be coming up. Ten hours had passed in what seemed like no time at all.

Had I gone to sleep? Certainly that was the most obvious explanation. But I didn't feel drowsy, had no sense of having opened my eyes to wake up. Besides, I find it impossible to sleep outside, even under the most pleasant conditions. Perhaps I'd been in a trance of some kind, an altered state induced by the retreat. If so, there was nothing hypnotic or ecstatic about it. The meditation technique I'd been practicing was not designed to put the mind in a trance. For the next few days I played with explanations. But finally I had to accept that I didn't know where the missing hours had gone. I'd just been sitting there with no verbal aware-ness, no words to give time and space the shape I'd known since the day I was born.

When I told my Zen teacher about it a week later, I was disappointed with his response. He offered no explanation. Instead he nodded slightly and told me to keep meditating each morning and attending retreats whenever I could. I'd been hoping he would tell me that I'd taken a crucial step in my Zen practice, that I'd had a rare glimpse of the unconditioned reality that exists outside the verbal cage of perception. But even before

I saw my teacher, I was skeptical of my desire to make what happened on the mountain seem more significant than it really was. If anything, my years of practicing Zen had taught me to question the imagery of visionary experience, distancing myself not just from mainstream religious teachings, but also from those mystical and esoteric traditions that supposedly offer a more authentic approach to the unknowable.

But something told me that those ten missing hours were important, that I shouldn't just dismiss them. I wanted to believe that if I could recover that gap in time, approach it without reducing it to conventional description, I might be making a serious contribution to a new kind of mystical practice, something that had nothing to do with religious doctrines of any kind. I had no intention of developing my own system of belief. I had long since outgrown the arrogant assumption that the universe can be systematically understood. In fact, I was convinced that far more harm than good had come from religious leaders who thought they knew what others ought to be thinking and doing. What appealed to me about Zen was its technique of destabilizing human arrogance, humbling its practitioners by leading them into radical uncertainty, relentlessly making them see that any assumption they might make about anything, no matter how logical or factual it seemed, was nothing more than a verbal house of cards.

But my own verbal house of cards collapsed when I got angry at my teacher's reaction. I hated the smug little smile that accompanied what he said. I knew he was only doing his job, that a Zen teacher needs to keep forcing people to question their thoughts and perceptions, especially when they show signs of becoming attached to what they believe. But I thought his dismissal was too formulaic, too automatic, that he should have explored what I said before he told me to forget it. Though at the time I tried to set my irritation aside, I found it increasingly difficult to meditate at the Zen center and attend the teacher's dharma talks.

Instead, I began taking long walks through a part of San Diego I didn't normally visit, a neighborhood that was mostly abandoned brick factories and warehouses, with a few huge old houses on the verge of collapsing. On one of these walks, I bumped into someone standing on a corner. I quickly apologized, but before I could take another step I got the distinct impression that I would see him two more times, the first time by choice and the second time without knowing it. He was otherwise non-descript. He might have been over a hundred years old and might have been only twenty. He nodded at the book in my hand, Basho's *Narrow Road to the Deep North*, a Zen classic that obliquely suggests that walking aimlessly can become a kind of meditative practice. He said he knew Basho's book backwards and forwards, especially backwards. I started to laugh, but he wasn't smiling. I didn't want to laugh at someone trying to be serious, so I put a serious look on my face. But I knew he knew I was faking it, so I decided I'd better express my true feelings, and I was just about to laugh, when I realized that laughter was no longer the authentic response. The lack of authentic response erased the previous ten seconds, and I felt like a film running backwards, moving back to the initial impulse to laugh, only this time I heard him say that he knew Basho's book backwards and forwards, but he stopped without saying especially backwards, which cancelled the laughter again.

I didn't want to keep standing there looking baffled, so I mentioned my experience on the mountain. He nodded eagerly, then looked at his watch and said he was late for work. I was turning to walk away when he asked me to come to his house the next day to talk further, pointing to a dirty white frame house wedged between brick factories at the end of the street. I told him nothing could keep me away.

But something almost did. Though I'd seen his house, written down his address, and walked up and down the street where he lived many times in the past few weeks, I lost my way, convinced that all the streets in the neighborhood looked alike. I'd never had this impression before. In fact, the main reason I liked walking there was that it was one of the few areas in San Diego where each street had its own character. Nonetheless, I got so lost that I was about to give up and go home, cursing myself for not having gotten his phone number. Then suddenly I was in front of his house, and he was standing in the doorway smiling, assuring me that everyone who came to his house got lost.

The front door opened into a dark wood corridor about fifty feet long. My shoes were pleased that the floor was polished wood. At the end of this corridor, we turned right, moving down another dark wood corridor, this one filled with identical black-and-white photographs of a crescent moon above a snow-capped mountain. At the end of this corridor, we turned right again, moving down yet another dark wood corridor, this one slanting up then slanting down then slanting side to side. At the end of this corridor, we turned right again, moving down yet another dark wood corridor, this one filled with whispered conversations about the ocean floor. At the end of this corridor, we turned right again, moving down yet another dark wood corridor, this one filled with the sound of people coughing, suddenly replaced by the sound of a pile of coins dropped on a glass countertop. At the end of this corridor, we turned right again, moving down yet another dark wood corridor, this one slightly shorter than the others, leading me toward a burst of barely suppressed idiotic laughter, as if I'd suddenly seen myself in a microscopic future, in corridors built by people the size of amoebas. At the end of this corridor, we turned right again, moving down yet another dark wood corridor, this one half as long as the one before it, with skylights on the floor and sky-blue carpeting on the ceiling. At the end of this corridor, we turned right again, moving down yet another dark wood corridor, this one slightly shorter than the one before it, and I felt my mouth opening as if I were going to speak, but instead I shortened my stride, compensating for the distance we'd been losing. At the end of this corridor, we turned right again, moving down yet another dark wood corridor, this one half as long as the one before it—so short, in fact, that it appeared to be twice as wide as the previous corridor, making it seem that the passage of time was on both sides of us, instead of behind and in front of us. At the end of this corridor, we turned right again, moving down yet another dark wood corridor, this one leading us back to the open front door.

He said: I've had a wonderful time. When can you come again?

I said: I don't mean to be rude, but I've been here less than five minutes.

He said: Actually, you've been here since noon— or maybe 12:15, since you were delayed. And now it's almost time for dinner.

I looked at him in disbelief and said: I might have been confused when I got here, but I wasn't *that* confused. I know I've been here five minutes at the most.

He smiled: Everyone gets that impression. But look at the sky if you don't believe it's almost time for dinner.

The sun was going down behind the factory smokestacks, and the late March sky was darkening. Clearly, it was almost time for dinner. I apologized and tried to look sheepish, but he just laughed and repeated that all his visitors left with the impression of having been there only five minutes.

I said: So how do you account for that? How do you—

He said: When can you come again?

I felt strange. But I didn't want things to get even stranger, so I smiled and offered to come the following Friday.

He said: That's what I thought you'd say. I'm looking forward to it.

He went inside and closed the door.

At first I tried to make light of what had just happened, telling myself that my sense of time had somehow become distorted. I got a cheap digital watch at the corner drugstore. But as I reviewed the experience, I became convinced that I was in the grip of something more ominous than temporal dislocation, that my sanity wouldn't be safe unless I went back to doing Zen in a supervised way.

My teacher was pleased when I returned. But when I described my recent encounter, he simply asked me what I made of it. I asked him what he made of it. He asked me why I cared more about what he made of it than what I made of it. I told him that I assumed his interpretations carried more Zen authority than mine. He said that Zen authority was a contradiction in terms. He gave me a very faint smile that told me the interview was over. Again, it was all I could do to contain my annoyance.

I wanted to slam the door as I left, violating what felt at the time like a pseudo-sacred environment. But I almost never express anger in such outwardly hostile ways, and the rage I repressed became a series of imagined slamming doors that led me to wander. Soon I found myself in a canyon filled with tall trees and abundant vegetation, a rare environment for San Diego. I was thinking about recent events in Washington, how thrilled I'd been a few days before when BITE, a group of activist poets, tried to assassinate President Bush. There was something absurd about writers trying to manage the tactical complexities of an assassination, but there was also something appropriate about it, since Bush, by his very presence, represented the death of the progressive imagination. Even though their plan had backfired and all of them were now in jail, their efforts had inspired billions of people all over the world.

BITE had also written an essay, emailing it to major newspapers across the country just a few minutes before their attempt to save the nation. The following day, right beside many front page accounts of the President's narrow escape from death, BITE's essay appeared in full, insisting quite convincingly that no U.S. President had ever been more deserving of assassination, claiming that their actions should not be classified as murder but as justifiable homicide. The time to bark was past; it was time to BITE, a name that was not an acronym but a verb. Predictably, millions of Americans were enraged. Talk of terrorist violence filled the airwaves. But a friend of mine who knew the editors of several radical magazines told me they were planning to publish lengthy reviews of BITE's essay, calling it a marvelous piece of argumentation, a text whose authenticity was obvious in every word, especially since in this case actions had spoken much louder than words.

But Bush was still President, and Republicans still had all the power. Something else had to be done. The BITE poets had called for others to follow in their footsteps, in the likely event that their plan failed. I'm sure I wasn't the only person who felt called upon to take action. My plans would have gone beyond the removal of President Bush, also targeting Cheney, Rumsfeld, and top-ranking Republican congressmen. But I knew I lacked the courage to become the next assassin. Though I had many good qualities, the ability to take decisive actions under pressure wasn't one of them.

Had I told my Zen teacher what I was thinking, he would have praised me for being unable to construct a plan and pull the trigger, insisting that violence was never the way, that it always just led to more violence and never solved anything. I would have said that extreme conditions call for extreme measures. Killing abusive Republican leaders was not just a sacred action but a sacred responsibility. He would have looked down, shaken his head slightly, looked up at me with a twinkle in his eyes and sent me away with that condescending smile.

The thought of my teacher brought me back to the present, the canyon of trees bending ever so slightly in the breeze. I looked at my new watch and saw that it was three o'clock on the dot. I heard the screech of a hawk, gliding in circles fifty feet above me. I always love watching these birds ride the updrafts and downdrafts, searching for prey, though it occurred to me that if I were a rabbit or mouse that mesmerizing motion might mean death. The circles were getting smaller and smaller, closer and closer. Then the hawk dove straight down, driving its flashing beak into my forehead, thrusting and thrashing its way into my head and neck and chest, replacing me in my body. I felt like the dot of an *i* released and climbing into the sky, riding the updrafts and downdrafts, scanning the ground for a meal, until I saw my body fifty feet below, looking up and watching me with my outspread wings in the circling sky, with each turn gliding lower and lower, then diving and driving a flashing beak into my forehead, thrusting and thrashing back into my body, stumbling at first, pausing to make sure everything was in place, then walking as quickly as possible, driven by a savage thirst. I took a short cut out of the canyon, stopped at the first convenience store I could find, bought a Coke, and drank it in ten seconds. Then I went home and stared at the floor for several hours, until I felt normal. But for the next two weeks, at precisely 3 p.m., I felt wings in my head and blinding pain in my forehead, as if the universe were violently struggling to rip open my third eye.

I found this feeling especially unnerving when I tried to meditate. I felt like a blank piece of paper trying to stop someone from making an illustration. I had nothing in theory against illustrations, but the similarity between illustration in the sense of making a picture and illustration in the sense of presenting an example began to upset me. I didn't want to be an example of anything. I didn't want to be part of a pattern emerging, with connections forming themselves to turn recent events into a narrative or discussion, a schematic picture that would then be a means of making sense of future events, forcing them to take the shape of meaning, domesticating the unknown. I remembered my teacher repeatedly asking me what I *made* of what was happening. I had taken his words in their customary sense, not examining the implications of the word *making*, not realizing that he was asking me to question my need to make anything, reminding me that all experience is unconsciously edited, arranged according to patterns built into our organs of perception. My goal in Zen meditation was to become aware of those patterns, to watch them as they came from the blank wall I was facing, and over time to make them less automatic, less unconscious. I knew that I would never leave them behind entirely. But it did seem possible to diminish my attachment to them, to become aware of them before they shaped my thought and behavior.

Indeed, this was already happening. Slowly over the past ten years, I'd been learning not to identify myself with the person I'd always told myself I was. From a Buddhist perspective, the right things were happening, even though I kept getting in my own way, falling back from time to time into predictable self-constructions. Progress was always unsteady, incremental. After all, I'd spent years developing an elaborate picture of myself, at times employing whatever professional help I could afford. Now that picture was being erased, and I felt like a crude enclosure made of cinder blocks and fake wood paneling, ten square feet of shade in a desert that kept getting hotter and larger. Of course, the figurative terms I was using were misleading, spatializing a transformation that had no spatial dimension. I needed to be patient, not so eager to put things into words.

But things without words were like the moon becoming an amoeba, a simile that lost an *i* to become a smile, a face that haunted my sleep for weeks. I wasn't in the grip of recurring dreams. The stories in which the face appeared were always different, apparently told by someone who couldn't or wouldn't stop changing the subject, as if the subject was change itself, though I saw the same face each night, knew it wasn't mine, and knew that when I woke up I wouldn't know whose face it was. Over time, the face became less distinct, until one night it was only a set of teeth, gleaming and receding, making the dark seem deeper and darker. I wanted to see how far it would go, to see how deep the darkness was, but the daily paper thumped at my neighbor's door, and I woke up in time to look out the window and see the paperboy rushing away, dropping the pile of papers under his arm, stopping to pick them up, then dashing around the corner, leaving his hat in the air behind him.

I often page through my neighbor's paper because I don't want to bother buying one myself. She sleeps until noon, and I get up at least an hour before dawn, so my habit of reading her paper outside her door, glancing at a few top news stories and getting the weather, never prevents her from finding her paper right where she expects it to be. But now, as I flipped through the pages, I noticed a small article about a group of standing stones discovered three days before on a Baja peninsula cliff, two hundred miles southeast of San Diego. According to the article, the stones were more than ten thousand years old, and similar in size and arrangement to Stonehenge, though at least five thousand years older. Since it seemed like an important discovery, I couldn't see why it wasn't front-page news. Had the archaeologists that discovered it made sure it was downplayed in the papers, wanting to avoid the consequences of publicity?

I'd been to that part of the Baja several times, and it's essentially uninhabited, a great place to be by yourself and watch dolphins play in the waves. So I got in my car and drove south. Once I got past the noise and congestion of the northern Baja cities, the ocean views were spectacular. The sunrise behind the mountains, spreading its colors over the changing shapes of purple clouds, was so lovely that I almost drove off the road several times. I thought about how I seemed to be caught in a sequence of strange events leading me to some definite conclusion, as if the universe were trying to show me something. I remembered that one of my closest friends had been led to join a satanic cult through a similar sequence of events, all in some way involving the number ten. I'd always thought he'd gone mad. But when I heard that he'd secretly been one of BITE's founding members and one of the chief architects of the plan to kill President Bush, I gained a new respect for devil worship.

The newspaper story had not disclosed the stones' exact location, but once my odometer told me that I'd gone two hundred miles, I turned off onto a small dirt road that wound between coastal hills and finally ended up near a cliff overlooking the sea. I left my car and walked south along a narrow trail. Fifteen minutes later, the path cut between two hills and opened into a large clearing. There, about fifteen feet from the edge of a cliff, were the stones I was looking for.

The papers had mentioned Stonehenge, and the similarity was impossible to miss. I'd been to Stonehenge thirty years before, in my early twenties, and though I'd been disappointed by the mob of tourists I'd had to contend with, the stones had made a strong impression on me. Now I had my own private Stonehenge. I knew of course that within a few months, the hills would be blasted away, the path would be enlarged and paved, a parking lot would be built, publicity campaigns would be launched, and the place would become just one more tourist attraction, complete with chartered busses, t-shirts, and colorful brochures. Any sacred or mysterious feeling about the place would be destroyed, absorbed into the busy noise of mainstream information. But for now the place was mine. The moment was perfect. The stones towered above me, transfigured by the morning light, which came in gold and silver bursts through cracks in surging clouds, flashing on the sea, the sound of waves one hundred feet below. I wanted to be in a trance, to feel myself dissolving into the stones, the solid pattern of energy in each individual stone and the patterns of energy all the stones made as a group, positioned in precise relation to each other and in relation to the place, the meeting point of land and sea.

I was familiar with the theories about Stonehenge —as a place where human sacrifice had been performed, as a cultural center, as an astronomical observatory, as a Neolithic calendar, as a huge image visible to inter-planetary beings approaching from the sky. But as I sifted through these possibilities, convinced that the best way to think about Stonehenge was as a repository of misconceptions, I remembered that I wasn't at Stonehenge, that the place I was visiting had not yet been assimilated into the narratives of human understanding. Despite its close resemblance to the famous stones in southern England, it may have served a very different purpose. I knew experts would speculate that the similarity between the two sites indicated that the same people had built them for the same reason, that southern England and the Baja peninsula had been populated by the same ancient culture, and that the stones had been taken from the same sacred mountain, establishing sites of magic power on opposite sides of the world. I thought I could feel the sacred current passing through the center of the earth, connecting me with another version of myself standing in southern England, wondering why the present moment felt like it was somewhere else. But this possibility faded in the gathering suspicion that it was only the meditative embrace of my gaze that was keeping the scene together, that with any lapse in my attention the place would crumble, darting off like startled fish in a thousand different directions.

This feeling quickly passed. The flashing sea, the erratic brilliance of the sky, the stillness of the stones, the accumulation of uncertainties—all combined to give the scene the evocative power of a painting in a gallery being looked at by several people, all of them quite moved and eager to talk about their feelings, which would have been fine, except that such discussions often become fierce arguments, and I didn't want anyone else's thoughts right now, especially not in the form of an intellectual debate. I wanted my own impressions, my own raw connection with the scene. So I turned and quickly walked back to my car, driving north.

But apparently I'd already stayed too long. The stones had become a gallery picture, a reflection of the people observing it, fading into a discussion they were having in a dim café, and as everyone kept changing the subject the picture was forgotten, leaving me with a blank space that was quickly filled with the impression of having taken a lovely drive up and down the Baja coastal road, looking in vain for a great restaurant a friend had recommended, a small place overlooking the sea, where the owner's husband was a powerful shaman, as well as being a legendary cook of Mexican breakfasts.

During the late sixties, hippies and anthropologists began to hold shamans in great esteem, rejecting the Euro-western mindset that had made shamans appear to be psychotics, trapped in delusional states filled with hallucinated encounters with spirits and the underworld. With the New Age movement of the 1980s, shamanism became fashionable. It was often assumed that all Native Americans were shamans, and people took weekend workshops at holistic centers, hoping to become shamans themselves. The New Age soon got old, but mainstream interest in shamanism continued. I knew this from my own professional experience, since the year before I'd made good money editing and producing a book called *Shamanism for Dummies*. In fact, I was still living off the sizeable sum I'd been paid for that assignment, the most I'd ever made in my fifteen years as a freelance editor.

I don't mean to make shamanism itself sound fake. But there's something dubious about the assumption that an esoteric discipline like shamanism can be truly understood outside of its cultural context. I had similar questions about Zen, which may have been why I'd never been fully convinced by my own involvement with it, or even by my American teacher's practice, despite the fact that he'd studied with well-known Japanese masters and had been meditating for more than forty years. The question was simple: What kind of spiritual authenticity was possible in a country dominated by shallow consumer ecstasies, a country where power-hungry people like Donald Trump, Steve Jobs, and Rupert Murdoch were called visionaries and sixty million people could decide that a dangerous clown like George W. Bush was not only a serious Christian but a good national leader? In such a degraded context, it seemed to me that sacred experience was possible only among individuals who had disciplined themselves to resist the contamination of mass imagery and information, creating media-free zones for themselves in their minds and hearts and homes. How many people in America could even begin to fit this description?

Among my friends I could think of only two. One of them was now in jail, facing what I assumed would be a life sentence, since he proudly acknowledged his part in trying to cleanse the nation of President Bush. The other friend had called me from New York a week before, announcing that he not only wanted but *needed* to visit me, a guy who had reached the age of sixty without ever holding a full-time job. He'd gotten rid of his first name because he liked being called Moon, his family name, and most people who knew him would have agreed that he was driven by lunar tendencies. He'd spent most of his adult life writing one long poem, an endless series of juxtaposed fragments written in response to an ancient book he'd found in his grandfather's attic. I'd seen the book several times. On each page was a woodcut featuring a mythic animal of some kind—a unicorn, manticore, gryphon, or one of many other strange creatures whose names I didn't know. The book apparently did more for Moon than it did for me. My interest was mainly in its age and the role it had played in his grandfather's life. But there was no publication information of any kind, no way to tell how old it was, and Moon had no recollection of his grandfather ever reading it. He didn't know how it ended up in the attic.

But the book was indispensable for his poem. Each of Moon's fragments was a response to one of the book's pages, not a description or commentary, but rather an improvisation based on the energy Moon took from the image. Why did images that struck me as having only historical value generate such powerful verbal moments for him? There was no way to know. But the evidence was incontestable. Moon's poem was more than mere poetry. It was language in its most visionary sense, conjuring its own worlds, refusing to subordinate itself to the so-called realistic task of describing or addressing what people had been trained to call society or nature. Though Moon had made no careerist moves to keep in touch with any of the poetry scenes that surrounded him on the Lower East Side of Manhattan, anyone who'd seen fragments of his epic knew that it was as challenging and strange as any innovative text of the early twenty-first century. Yet in some ways it felt as old as *The Epic of Gilgamesh*.

I wanted to keep thinking about Gilgamesh, the incantatory depiction of his ten-day journey into the mountain at the end of the world. But people were honking at me. My driving was apparently worse than usual, and I told myself to concentrate on the road. Fortunately, I'd already crossed the border and wasn't far from my apartment. As I parked in front of the small building I lived in, I noticed the newsboy's hat, still suspended in the air where he'd left it behind ten hours before. This reminded me of the article I'd read that morning, and I was trapped between vague recollections—the standing stones and my failed attempts to find the shaman's restaurant—memories that both seemed uncertain, precisely the feeling Moon claimed he received from the images in his magic book.

I went inside and looked at the calendar on my kitchen wall, where I'd made a note of Moon's arrival later that week. It was more than a social visit, he'd assured me over the phone, claiming that his poem had led him to realize that there was someone he had to meet in the desert east of San Diego. Part of me was amused by this cryptic mission. It sounded so theatrical, as if Moon thought of himself as a Biblical prophet responding to commands from the great beyond. But another part of me was moved by Moon's dedication. Here he was—a sixty-year-old man—hitchhiking three thousand miles from New York City, all because of what words on a page were telling him!

He arrived in the middle of the night and collapsed without a word on my living room sofa. I couldn't wake him until sundown the following day. When he finally got up his eyes were filled with fire, and he quickly explained that he'd needed the sleep not just because he was exhausted, but because it would have been dangerous to open his eyes before his dreaming was completed. Without asking me how I was or what my plans were, he insisted that we had to leave at dawn the following day. I knew better than to argue with him. But when he told me I should meditate all night in preparation, I had to say something.

I tried to sound casual: Listen, Moon, the meditation I do doesn't prepare me for anything. If anything, it's a way of making sure I'm not prepared.

He said: What good does it do you to be unprepared?

I said: What good does it do you to read poetry you're not prepared to understand? If you're not prepared, you can have a real reaction.

He said: Fine. But you need to do something to gather and focus your energy. You're going to need everything you've got in the desert tomorrow.

When I asked him why, he shrugged and asked me to get him a glass of water. Then he asked me about the book on shamanism someone had apparently told him I'd written. I quickly explained that it was just an editing job I'd done for money. He gave me a strange look, somewhere between contempt and amazement, then said he needed to take a walk by himself and quickly left. At first I was baffled. Was it really so terrible that I'd done some editing work to pay my bills? Then I remembered stories Moon's ex-girlfriend had told me about the years he'd spent in Mexico in the early seventies, right before he moved to New York and began his poem. Apparently he'd had contact with a Huichol shaman in the central Mexican highlands and had been clinically insane when he came to New York, lapsing into extended bouts of laughter for no apparent reason. The poem had been his way of putting his mind back together. Maybe that explained the look he'd given me. Maybe he'd been shocked that someone could calmly make money off something that had driven him out of his mind. But when he came back two hours later he showed no signs of hostility. Instead he asked me about my Zen practice, seemed interested in the answers I gave him, then said he felt tired and needed to go back to sleep.

When we woke before dawn the following day, I was eager to talk about the pattern of strange events I'd been caught up in. I figured if anyone could shed some light on what was going on, it was Moon. But he was clearly preoccupied, so we drove in silence into the desert. We stopped for food and water near the southern end of the Salton Sea, about seventy miles northeast of San Diego, then went south another twenty-five miles. We stopped at the end of a long dirt road and walked for perhaps an hour, following a rough trail through a rocky labyrinth of hills and canyons, finally arriving at a crude enclosure made of cinder blocks and fake wood paneling. Its occupant was a man who might have been over a hundred years old and might have been only twenty. He seemed to know my face. His face was like a door standing all by itself in the middle of nowhere.

After talking with Moon for a few minutes in a language I didn't recognize, he went back inside. Moon told me to sit and wait. I rested my back on a smooth rock in the shadow of a mesa, looking west at Garnet Peak, wondering if the hawks that rode the winds at the summit were feasting on the ten hours I'd lost there.

I don't know how long we waited, somewhere between ten minutes and ten hours. My teeth felt like they'd been gone for a long time but had somehow gotten back into my mouth before I knew they were missing. Then the man was standing outside his hut in a costume that made him look like a huge bird of prey, something between a hawk and an owl. I wanted to laugh but something stopped me. Moon made a fire in a pile of round white stones. The smell was delicious, as if the stones were the homes of secret aromas that could only be released by fire. Moon held up two flat wooden objects and told me we would be using them as drums. He showed me the beat and told me to keep it steady. The man began dancing, spinning in slow circles, each one part of a larger circle, chanting in a language I didn't know.

At first I felt silly. I looked at Moon and shrugged. But the sharp look he gave me made me feel stupid, and soon the beat and the chant and the dance began to absorb my attention. The word "absorb" is not a figure of speech. The world slowly contracted into the dance, became the dance, and before too long I was nothing more than a vehicle of the rhythm I was making with my drum, and the drum was time itself but without human measurement, not gliding across the surface of the world, but slowly beating its way into the depth of space, dissolving into colors and shapes, velocities and textures. The only way to describe the dance was to say that it came from the sun, just as the chant was coming from a hawk in the circling sky, gracefully riding the updrafts and downdrafts, as if it might suddenly dive and drive its beak deep into my forehead.

But then the hawk was gone. Our drumming stopped. The man collapsed. He lay motionless by the fire, and Moon knelt beside him, posing what seemed to be questions, again in a language I'd never heard before. The phrases felt like a system of corridors constructed only to break down the distinction between arriving and departing, as if each corridor were a missing interval of time, parts of a house that existed only on the outside, a place that no one approached without getting lost.

Moon finally nodded, stood and smiled at me with burning eyes. I could feel my back leaning on a smooth rock, cold at first then hot then made of circles. The pain that had been mounting behind my eyes began to relax, like music breaking out of a buried coffin. Moon went into the hut and came out with a knife. He put the blade in the fire, then kneeled and made a quick incision, pulling open the man's chest and stomach. He motioned for me to bring him an old wicker basket beside the hut. One by one, Moon pulled out the man's internal organs, placing them carefully in the basket, replacing them with the burning stones. He motioned for me to close the basket and place it back inside the hut. Then he pulled the man's body back together, sealing it with the wave-like motions of his hands.

We started drumming again, and soon the man was up and dancing, this time shouting with ecstasy at the sun going down behind Garnet Peak. The words of his chant had such presence that they didn't vanish right after they came from his mouth. Rather, they drifted up like vapors, shaping themselves into cumulonimbus clouds, disappearing over the mountains, as if they were crossing a threshold into another dimension. It occurred to me that in this other dimension, every place was the same place, and words were things and things were words. Then it occurred to me that this thought was foolish. Then it occurred to me that it was no more foolish than anything else people thought about other dimensions. Then it occurred to me that I didn't really know what a dimension was, that probably no one else did either. Then it occurred to me that each thing that occurred to me occurred to me so that other things might occur me. Then it occurred to me that I was trapped in things that occurred to me. Then the word occur became five stones that marked the edge of the space the man made with his dance—but north was facing west, south was facing east, and the fifth direction, which I wanted to call the center, was never the same, changing with the dance and the beat and the chant and the heat of the sun, whose beams came raining down in spears and arrows, marking the dust, as if the desert had once been a sequence of pages, and before that, an ocean of words on the verge of becoming a language, and before that, the collection of one-celled animals that became those words, and before that, a random set of chemical reactions, and before that, the musical score those chemicals emerged from, and before that, the word *that* becoming *before* becoming *and*, as if there was nothing before that *and*, and the man was chanting louder, slicing the air with large white feathers, cutting space into words that the gathering wind was whirling away. For a second I knew precisely what they meant, and then I knew nothing, like a bubble of air rising rapidly from the ocean floor, bursting once it reached the air on the surface.

Again the man collapsed and our drumming stopped. With his bare hands, Moon pulled open the man's body, removed the burning stones, and motioned for me to bring the basket, carefully putting the man's internal organs back into his body. Then he closed him up, massaging his skin, again making wave-like motions with his hands, leaving no trace of the opening he'd made. Ten minutes later the man slowly got up, gazed at the gash in the sky where the sun had gone down behind Garnet Peak, nodded to Moon and me, and disappeared into his hut.

Then Moon and I were stumbling and weaving our way back out through the desert night. As I drove toward San Diego, he sat gazing out the window, refusing to speak, as if he were there by himself, as if he were someone I no longer knew. When we got home, he aggressively steered the conversation toward things we'd done together thirty years before in New York City, and our laughing memories seemed to intrude on and transform what had just happened in the desert. It's no secret that memory is more a reconstruction than it is an objective account of past events, but our conversation made my recollections even more unstable, and later that night, after Moon had gone to bed, I was sure that what I remembered was quite different from what really took place. I knew that if I told my Zen teacher about it, he would give me that slightly condescending smile and tell me not to put so much emphasis on the paranormal side effects of my practice. So I decided to keep the experience to myself.

Moon left the next day, resisting all my requests for an explanation, except to say that our work in the desert had been crucial in restoring the health of the nation. I'd always felt that to talk about *restoring* the nation's health was misguided, implying that the United States had at some point in its past been truly healthy. But exactly ten days later, the nation was buzzing with what the media called a tragic disaster, even though it made me happier than I'd been in many years. It was either a marvelous coincidence or the result of a magical process I couldn't begin to understand. Had someone predicted it the day before, I would have laughed.

But there it was in the headlines of every paper I looked at, on every TV newscast, on radios and the Internet. George Bush was dead. Dick Cheney was dead. Donald Rumsfeld was dead. Karl Rove was dead. All the leading Republicans on Capitol Hill were dead. All the Republican think-tank people were dead. The immediate assumption was that terrorists had somehow been responsible. But not a single person had been murdered. Bush had been struck by lightning on his ranch, and the rest had died of strokes, heart attacks, aneurisms, and freeway accidents—all within the same ten-hour period. Meanwhile, the White House had been occupied by environmental activists, apparently with Pentagon approval.

Of course, I thought of Moon, his claim about our actions in the desert. But when I tried to reach him by phone, his ex-girlfriend answered instead. She told me Moon had changed his name and moved out of his apartment, claiming that within ten days his book would come to an end, and everyone he'd ever known would forget they'd ever known him.

# CELL

I couldn't stand the cell phones any longer. I couldn't stand the swarms of people with phones pressed up to their ears, eyes bright with hi-tech happiness, walking and talking endlessly about nothing. When I started amusing myself by calling them "phonies," even though I'd always avoided such terms of contempt in the past, I knew I needed a change. So I took my dog and drove out into the desert, planning to stay away as long as I could.

Two hours east of the city, I came to a town I'd been to several times before. But everyone there had cell phones, so I knew I had to go further. I drove east another two hours and came to a town I'd never seen on a map, a place where all the buildings seemed to be more than a hundred years old. I parked and watched the people going up and down the town's main street. For more than an hour, I didn't see any cell phones. It looked like I was in the right place. At first I thought I should find a hotel, but I wasn't ready to be around other people, so I drove thirty miles out of town, found a hiking trail, and started walking.

The desert was filled with canyons and mesas, ringed with towering mountains. It felt good to walk with my dog in a silence broken only by the cries of circling hawks and the sound of wind. There was no need to think about what I'd left behind or what I might be doing in the future. There was no need to do anything but enjoy what I was looking at. I felt like radio music finally arriving without any static. The more I walked the better I felt. The sky was blue enough to drink. But finally I needed shelter from the sun, so I called my dog and we sat in the shade of a huge rock. I poured water into the small plastic bowl I keep in my backpack, and my dog drank it quickly. Then something caught his attention and he took off down a steep slope into a canyon.

I sat and stared into the distance. Thirty minutes passed. The words that were telling me what I was thinking went backwards. The same thirty minutes passed again. The words that were telling me what I was thinking went backwards. The same thirty minutes passed again. For less than a second I became a tall cactus on a ridge thirty yards to my left. I saw myself sitting with my dog in the shade of a huge rock, staring at the sky. The words that were telling me what I was thinking went backwards. The same thirty minutes passed again. The wind was picking up and getting colder. The sun was about to go down behind a mountain, at least one hour too soon for a late March sunset. My dog still hadn't come back. I called him three times. His name echoed only the second time. There was no sign of him. I knew I had to find him before the sun went down. I took a long drink of water from the bottle in my pack. Then I stumbled down into the canyon.

The canyon floor was a labyrinth of tall blade-like rocks and jagged shadows. I started walking toward what I thought was my dog barking in the distance, but it turned out to be the stiff wind amplified and distorted by the rocks and walls of the canyon. The wind kept getting louder, blowing sand into my face, forcing me to take shelter behind a rock. The shadows were getting longer and I knew I had to get out. But I couldn't leave my dog in the canyon all night. Finally I decided to go back to my car and get a flashlight. I stumbled through the gathering darkness up the steep side of the canyon. The stars were coming out in the deepening twilight. When I got back to my car, my dog was sitting there placidly chewing a bone. He looked up at me and wagged his tail as if nothing had happened.

We drove back into town. I stopped for gas and then went into a small café for dinner. The only other customer was wearing black robes and a conic black magician's hat. He was eating a double cheeseburger with French fries and a Coke. The waitress came and asked me what I wanted. I ordered a double cheeseburger with French fries and a Coke.

I stared out the window onto the street, the dark line of brick buildings, all of which seemed to be empty, though jazz was playing from someone's open window. I looked at the man on the other side of the room. He was looking at me as if I should have known who he was. I looked back at him as if he should have known who I was. For less than a second, I felt like I was dressed as a magician. I knew the words of power. I knew all the shapes I could take.

The waitress brought my food. It was the best cheeseburger I'd ever tasted. The fries were perfectly crisp. I'd never had a better Coke. Soon after I finished, the waitress brought me another double cheeseburger with French fries and a Coke. My hunger had increased and the food was even better than before. Soon after I finished, the waitress brought me another double cheeseburger with French fries and a Coke. My hunger had increased and the food was even better than before. I looked at the man across the room. He met my eyes with silent laughter. Then he got up and left. The conversation we could have had hovered like fine mist about three inches above his empty plates.

The waitress was tall and thin, with long brown hair and glasses. She wore a blank white sweatshirt and faded blue jeans.

She said: Can I get you anything else?

I thought for a minute: No, I guess not. Just the check.

She smiled: How was your food?

I smiled back: Incredible.

She said: That's what everybody says.

I said: Why aren't there more people here? You make the best burgers on the planet. Why isn't the place packed?

She shrugged: Beats me. But I'm not complaining. The owner pays me pretty well even if no one shows up. And he lets me sit and read if there's no one to wait on. It's a good situation.

I said: Sounds like it. Does that guy who was here before come here often?

She said: Every night. And he always gets the same thing.

I said: Does he live here in town?

She seated herself at the table and said: I don't think so. I've never seen him anywhere but here. I live right across the street, and if he lived in town I'm sure I'd have seen him at some point during the day.

I said: Maybe the only place he exists is right here.

She looked at me in silence. The wind was rattling the windows. The clock on the wall had stopped at 3:15. She finally said: What's that supposed to mean?

I wasn't sure. So I smiled and said: I'm joking.

She said: I don't get it.

How was I going to explain? I wanted to get up and walk out. But something about the darkness of the wind prevented me from leaving.

She said: I really don't get it.

She looked impossibly serious. I knew I had to say something. But the pressure to speak was making speech impossible. I thought of changing the subject, but her face was telling me that evasive behavior of any kind would be unacceptable. I put my hands flat on the table and stared out the window, tracking the line of streetlights into the distance, watching them advancing and receding, a double motion so carefully balanced that nothing seemed to be moving. I looked back at my hands, flat on the table. I lifted them two inches, moved them two inches to the left and put them back down, lifted them two inches again, moved them back two inches to the right and put them back down.

I couldn't stand the silence anymore. I had to change the subject, so I said: The other day I saw that new townhouse condos were being sold a few blocks from where I live. It's not like I can afford a townhouse condo. But I wanted to see how much one of them cost. There was an open house so I went inside. They were fairly nice—three bedrooms, three baths, three floors, pretty good urban views from the top floor. But the rooms all looked like showrooms in a department store, fancy but totally boring. They cost a million dollars each. A million dollars! And it's not even a rich neighborhood. Can you imagine? And if you bought one of these places, you wouldn't even get a yard or a swimming pool.

She said: I *hate* swimming pools.

Something about the way her voice expanded around the word *hate* got me up from the table and out the door. I got in my car and drove like a maniac, running two stoplights. My dog was looking anxiously out the window, jumping into the back seat, pacing back and forth, jumping back into the front seat, whimpering softly. I stroked his head and scratched his ears, but he wouldn't calm down. The darkness on the edge of town had never been more inviting.

I wasn't sure where I was going. There were no road signs, and I had no map in the car. All I knew for sure was that before too long I was climbing, circling up into the mountains, and the air was getting colder. Soon I had to roll up my windows and turn on the heat. On either side of the road was a dense pine forest. I knew I should probably go back and ask for directions, but something about the hate in the woman's voice made the whole town seem sinister.

I thought of turning west and going home, but I knew there were cell phones there, and hundreds of other technological obsessions, many of them waiting in the future. I thought about how much I hated video games and automated answering systems, plasma TVs and digital cameras, shopping malls and subdivisions. Suddenly one woman's angry voice didn't seem so dangerous. But the night was parting in front of me, closing in back of me, as if it wanted me to keep moving. I felt powerless to resist. An hour passed without any road signs. The wind was getting harder and colder. Soon I began to see patches of snow in the forest. I knew I had to find a place to stop.

Finally I saw what looked like a driveway. I turned off and followed it more than a mile, until it stopped in front of a huge stone house, apparently uninhabited. My first impulse was to turn back, but I was getting too sleepy to drive, so I went to the front door and knocked as loud as I could. The door opened on its own. I stepped inside. The darkness felt like a series of transparent curtains, opening finally onto a broad staircase. To my left and right were doorways into large rooms filled with old furniture. I stumbled through the room to my left. The first thing I saw was a grand piano. I sat at the bench and banged on the keys. Instead of music, I heard laughter. Something told me to leave as fast as I could.

But something else told me to go upstairs. I went upstairs. All the rooms were furnished with the same combination of antique mirrors, dressers, and armchairs, with freshly made four-poster beds. I wanted to sleep. But the beds were so perfectly made, the sheets were so crisp and clean, that I felt I'd better sleep on the floor. In one of the rooms I found a small door, which didn't open into a closet, but onto a steep narrow staircase. I climbed into what I assumed would be an attic. But it turned out to be a large room with French windows looking out over an expanse of pines toward the moonlit snow of distant mountains. I collapsed into a small unmade bed, warming my freezing body with an old blanket I found stuffed under a battered armchair. I fell asleep in seconds.

All night I could hear the wind against the windows. At some point I heard a voice. I woke. The words continued. I sat up and quickly scanned the moonlit room. There was no one else there. The voice was clearly mine, but it wasn't coming out of my mouth. It was on the other side of the room, above the battered armchair, speaking like someone reading to himself, struggling with phrases and sentences that he couldn't seem to grasp at first, repeating some of them three or four times before moving on, a narrative about someone doing exactly what I'd done several hours before, driving away from a city into the desert, driving away from a café into the mountains, as if the house were haunted by the ghost of my immediate past. I was scared and wanted to get up and leave, but I forced myself to listen. The crescent moon in the window disappeared behind a cloud. Slowly the voice faded into the wind. I drifted back to sleep.

I woke early the next morning, opened a can of dog food for my dog, then got on the road, driving for hours down mountain roads, the landscape changing gradually from pine forest to desert scrub. Soon I was flooded with sunlight on a straight level road. I stepped on the gas and made good time, arriving for lunch in a town that seemed to be one street of old brick buildings. I found a small café and went inside. The man with the magician's hat sat at a corner table, eating a double cheeseburger with fries and a Coke. Slow jazz came from someone's open window. When the waitress appeared with long brown hair and a white sweatshirt, I ordered a chef's salad, but she brought me a double cheeseburger with fries and a Coke.

I said: Sorry, this isn't what I ordered.

She said: It's not?

I said: No. I ordered a chef's salad.

She said: That's not on the menu.

I said: Can I see the menu again?

She looked at her pad and said: I wrote your order down right here. You ordered the double cheeseburger platter.

I said: I'm sure I saw a chef's salad on the menu. Can I see the menu again?

She looked puzzled but nodded and smiled and went back into the kitchen. When she didn't come back right away, hunger got the best of me, and I quickly devoured the best double cheeseburger platter on the planet. She finally returned with another double cheeseburger platter. I got frantically hungry all over again and ate quickly, ecstatically. She soon returned with another double cheeseburger platter. I told myself I was eating too much too quickly. Instead of wolfing down more food, I thought I should try to talk to the magician. But he met my eyes again with silent laughter, and I looked away, back to the food on my plate. I felt frantically hungry. I ate quickly, ecstatically, and when I looked across the room again the magician was gone.

The waitress came back and said: Can I get you anything else?

I fought the urge to say *no, I guess not, just the check*. Instead I said: What's going on here?

She stood there with her mouth open, pencil poised above her pad. Finally she said: What do you mean?

I wasn't sure what I meant.

She said: What does *what's going on here* mean? You're in a small café. You ordered something for lunch.

I wanted to blurt out something about absurdly overpriced condos. I wanted to make her say that she *hated* swimming pools. I wanted to take the hate in her voice and fill it with vitamins and minerals, grind it up and put it in a can and sell it. But I knew that I hated swimming pools too, and though I told myself that the hate was the problem, I couldn't get myself to believe that anger and disgust were out of place, especially when I thought of all the happy self-important faces of people using cell phones. Who was I to turn away from someone whose only crime was that she bluntly expressed the contempt we both felt, the contempt we both felt any intelligent person would feel and want to express?

She tapped her pad with her pencil, cocked her head and said: You're in a small café. You ordered something for lunch.

I looked out into the fading light. Again the sun was going down too soon. According to my watch it wasn't even half past four. I looked at the waitress tapping her pad and cocking her head. I cocked my head

89

and started tapping my finger on the table. I tried to crease my brow so that I looked like I was thinking. I tried to tell myself what I was thinking. It wasn't easy. As soon as I put my thoughts into words, it felt like I'd replaced my thoughts with words, with sounds and shapes that had no firm connection with anything beyond their own sounds and shapes, defining themselves only in relation to each other.

I looked back outside. My car's windows were open. My dog had jumped out and was running down the road. I put a twenty-dollar bill on the table, excused myself and rushed out to my car. I drove as fast as I could but my dog seemed always to be the same distance away, a dot on a long white road, until he disappeared into the deepening twilight. I pulled off the road, got out and shouted my dog's name as loud as I could, over and over again. There was no response, just the echoes of his name. For the first time since I'd adopted him five years before, I felt alone. But I knew the only thing I could do was keep driving and hope for the best.

The road was climbing out of the desert into the mountains. The fading light was deceptive, the pavement increasingly icy. I felt that at any moment I might skid off the road and over the edge of a cliff. On the other side of the road was the forest, pines framing patches of snow that grew larger and more frequent as the road curved upward. The steady sound of the engine was making me sleepy, bringing me to the edge of a trance filled with shifting patterns of moonlight split by thousands of branches bending in the wind. To keep myself awake, I turned on the radio. The DJ said she was broadcasting from the moon, which I thought was a stupid joke, except that the music was unlike anything I'd ever listened to, resembling the motion of a box kite in the wind, erratically darting up and dodging side to side and diving, resembling the motion of a swing gliding up into a sunlit pause and gliding back down into shade, resembling the motion of a waterfall plunging and rising in faint prismatic mist, resembling the motion of an ambulance on a slippery mountain road, sliding up and down one steep switchback after another, resembling the motion of a lifeboat in a storm, lifted into the sky with each wave, trembling briefly in the foam of each crest, dropping quickly into the frothing dark before the next wave, analogies superimposed, each above and between and below the others, not moving and changing from moment to moment, but moving and changing into the depth of a single deepening moment, finally stopping in front of a huge stone house.

It looked at first like the house I'd slept in the night before. But when I circled it several times, peering through the windows, I saw that the rooms were empty, not filled with antique furniture. I knocked several times before going inside. I walked down what seemed like a long corridor filled with Dutch landscape paintings, though I could see that the walls were bare. Finally I came to a staircase. I went up slowly, pausing with each step, for some reason trying to count my way up, but mixing up the numbers. When I finally got to the landing, I walked straight into what looked in the dark like an open doorway, until I realized that I was stepping into a floor-length mirror, passing through my own reflection coming toward me. It felt like a split second of rain. Something told me to stop but I kept going, refusing to turn back and look at myself turning to look back from the other side of the glass. Even though I was now apparently functioning as a reflection—an unobserved reflection—it didn't make any difference. My footsteps made the same sound they always made on bare wood floorboards. I walked down the hallway to another flight of stairs, which spiraled up into a large room filled with moonlight.

I found a blanket in a closet and slept in a battered armchair facing open casement windows. When I woke the next morning, I felt afraid, like I might get in trouble for sleeping in a house that wasn't mine. I hurried downstairs and was shocked at first to see myself coming toward me. But then I remembered the mirror and passed again through my reflection. This time I turned and looked back at myself looking back, a split second of laughter.

Soon I was driving back down the mountain. Five thousand feet below, the desert floor stretched out for hundreds of miles. It looked so pure, so free of morons blabbing on cell phones. But something was wrong. If the desert floor was a page in a book, the words were having trouble holding the scene in place, suggesting that the late morning light pressing down on each object might just as well have been peeled off and folded up and used for something else.

I drove for a long time, hoping my dog would suddenly appear as a distant dot in the deep white space. I turned on the radio. A tragic voice caught between bursts of static announced that President Bush had been struck by lightning. I turned to another station. A tragic voice caught between bursts of static announced that President Bush had been struck by lightning. I turned to another station. A tragic voice caught between bursts of static announced that President Bush had been struck by lightning. I pulled over and got out. I lifted my arms to the sky and shouted with joy. For ten seconds, I believed that nature functioned according to moral principles. But then I remembered that good people often got killed in earthquakes, floods, tidal waves, and volcanic eruptions, while bad people routinely did horrible things without cosmic retribution. I also remembered that Bush had been in the White House for almost five years, and that if nature truly functioned according to moral principles, he would have been hit by lightning before he took office.

I looked at my watch. It was 2 p.m. Why was the sun going down? Why had the days gotten shorter? Where were the missing hours? Would the same thing keep happening as the days passed, until there was no time left at all? Was it up to me to invent the time that was missing? And if I failed to do so, would the disappearance of time mean that I too had vanished? It was too soon to tell. But it did seem clear that there had to be a connection between the rise of George Bush, the obsession with cell phones, and the sudden collapse of time. Was it too much to say that the world had become so stupid that there was no longer any reason to keep track of things, that time was vanishing because it had better ways to spend its time? The question circled above my head like a hawk in the desert sky, something I could only admire from a distance. I felt closer to the assumption that I was slowly giving myself up to a pattern of behavior and events that existed only because I was slowly giving myself up to it. No matter how limited such a world might be, it was better than being surrounded by people on cell phones.

I stopped for gas. I wanted to get a map but the convenience store was closed. I could see the lights of a town in the darkening distance. But when I got there everything was closed, perhaps because the president was dead. At the end of the main street, something moved in the dark. I called my dog's name and he came running, wagging his tail. He jumped into my car and I broke out a can of dog food. Then I saw that a light had come on down the street on the second floor of a brick building, and soon some kind of jazz was floating softly from an open window. I followed the music through a door beside an empty storefront, up a flight of stairs, and down a hallway to someone's apartment.

I knocked three times. There was no answer. I opened the door and stepped inside, prepared to make an awkward explanation. But the room was empty. I called out to see if anyone was home. No one answered. Jazz came from a CD player beside a bookshelf, on top of which I saw three tropical fish in an artfully furnished aquarium. Their graceful movements made the music even more graceful, and I realized that it wasn't jazz I was listening to, but the same lunar symphony I'd heard in my car the night before.

I went down a hallway past a kitchen where three hamburgers were frying in a skillet, came to a small dark bedroom and switched on the light, but no one was there. Just another bookshelf and a mattress on the floor, a pillow on top of a neatly folded blanket, a faded oval rug that looked like the earth photographed from the moon. I turned off the light and went back to the living room and sat on a futon couch. The music was enchanting, advancing and receding at the same time, making the distinction between the two motions obsolete, but the sound of food cooking in the kitchen distracted me. I got up and turned off the flame. Then I went back and sat and watched the fish and listened to the music. I've always liked music better in the dark so I turned off the light. Between the fluttering white silk drapes, the open window framed a half moon floating in the dark windows of old brick buildings across the street. The bubbling sound of the aquarium filter played with the gusting sound of the wind, as if they were parts of the music I was listening to.

Soon I got hungry. I turned the stove back on, waited a minute or two, got bread from the breadbox, and quickly gobbled up two delicious hamburgers. I took the third one outside and gave it to my dog. Then I brought him up into the apartment and he curled up on the floor and fell asleep. I found a bathroom down the hall and took a quick shower. The warm, relaxing water felt like music on the moon. I stretched out on the couch, covering myself with a blanket I took from a closet next to the bathroom. The cold wind playing in the drapes filled me with pleasure, which took the form of doubt: Had anything really happened? Had any of my encounters over the past few days been real? Had I been so devastated by the world of cell phones that my perceptions had been permanently deformed? Or was I rather about halfway into the process of recovering from a world so pathologically fake that partial unreality was the best my perceptions could do? There was no way to know for sure. But I did feel certain that *something* had to have happened, even if I wasn't sure what it was. And if what I remembered wasn't real, it was up to me to fill the emptied space those unreal places and actions occupied, to come up with alternatives to the recent past. But since those alternatives would also have been uncertain, nothing more than verbal constructions, I saw no reason to waste my time inventing them, which left me with no recourse but to accept what I now remembered, approaching its uncertainty with pleasure, much as the drapes accepted the wind that was tossing and shaping them.

I fell asleep slowly and pleasantly. At some point in the night I woke briefly to the sound of footsteps moving down the hall to the bedroom. But when I got up the next morning, the room was empty, looking precisely the way it looked the night before, except that the blinds in the window above the bed had been opened, offering a view of distant mountains above the housetops.

Monstrous noises came from the street. I rushed outside. At the western end of town, I saw wrecking machines at work, knocking down buildings. I stood there for ten minutes, watching in shock, as homes and bars and shops were reduced to piles of brick, splintered wood, dust and shattered glass. I wanted to find out why, so I walked down the street and signaled to a man driving a yellow bulldozer. He looked at me briefly, scowled, and went back to work. I called my dog and we drove out into the desert again.

I tried to get some local news on the radio. But between bursts of static, I heard nothing but voices tragically discussing the death of President Bush. Finally, at the far end of the dial, I heard something about plans to wipe a town off the map, but I couldn't get the name of the town or the reasons for its destruction. I told myself I should get a map, but the only store on the road was the place I'd stopped the day before, and it was still closed. The only thing to do was to keep going straight, hoping I could find another store and get a map. I wondered why I felt such a need for a map, why I wasn't just finding hiking trails and walking around and looking at things. If there wasn't really any place to go, why was I in such a hurry to get there? Was I still so hooked into the world of cell phones and computers that I needed to see where I was in relation to everything else? Was I afraid of being lost? I stepped on the gas and soon the road began climbing into the mountains.

On either side of the road there were giant boulders, so white and smooth they might have been huge eggs. I thought of huge predatory birds, hatching fully grown, sweeping over the desert and wreaking havoc on the civilized world. I imagined people with cell phones wandering through shattered streets talking endlessly about nothing, finally starving or dying of thirst, until there was only one person left blathering into a cell phone, the last human words on earth, with no one listening.

The sun was going down, even though it was only half past noon. I turned on the radio but there was nothing but static so I turned it off, turned it on ten minutes later, got nothing but static and turned it off again. My dog was sleeping peacefully beside me, not even slightly concerned that time was being carted off piece by piece. The sunset was a blaze of reds and golds on huge clouds changing in the wind. I felt like my car was about to get blown off the road, so I pulled over and got out. It was colder than I expected. I took a heavy coat from the trunk and got back inside. My dog woke up and watched the sunset for a few minutes, then put his head in my lap and went back to sleep. There was something so comforting about this that I felt no need to start the car and find a place to stay for the night, and as the clouds and colors faded slowly in the west, I fell asleep.

All night I could hear the wind slamming into my car. I felt afraid and woke up several times. But when

I felt my dog's head in my lap, the fear dissolved, and I went back to sleep. I woke at five. It was cold, so I started the engine and got on the road. I turned on the radio. Between bursts of static, I heard that Dick Cheney and Donald Rumsfeld were also dead, along with many Capitol Hill Republicans, and I wondered if they'd been hit by lightning too. But I couldn't get any more news. The static was blocking everything out.

Soon I was driving east and I could see the sky getting lighter. The road was still climbing, but after running east for half an hour, it leveled off and I knew I'd come to the top of the mountain. The predawn blue of the sky felt like a blue I'd seen more than half a century before, two thousand miles away. The sudden connection between times and places made the sky seem deeper, as if it were gazing back at me and feeling the same connection. I wanted to rest in that feeling forever. But suddenly the road was lined on both sides with old brick buildings.

I stopped, got out of the car, and walked up the street. There was no sign that anyone lived there. At the end of the street I turned right. There was nothing but rocks and scrub vegetation. I turned around and saw the same thing in the other direction. The town was only one street. And apparently not even that. From where I now stood, in back of the buildings, I could see they were flat, held up with blocks of wood, like painted stage props. As the sun began to rise, filling the street with light, my suspicions were confirmed: the town was unreal. I told myself it had to be an abandoned movie set, and sure enough, as I walked back down the street I saw something I'd missed before, an open three-ring binder with pages turning fiercely in the wind, apparently a screenplay, though most of it was missing.

I sat and read what remained, lines for characters named Phil and Connie, parts of a witty conversation about fall-out shelters in the early 1960s. I laughed at first, but soon I started getting angry, thinking back to the Cuban Missile Crisis, Kennedy's face on the picture tube making a speech, pushing the world to the brink of mass destruction. Then I thought about Bush and got even madder, especially since the radio fragments I'd heard the day before made it sound like Americans all over the nation were mourning his death, and now they were no doubt mourning the deaths of other Republican leaders. Why would anyone mourn for people whose actions had done so much to ruin the world? I was glad that I wasn't in touch with the rest of the nation.

At the other end of the street I came to a small café that seemed to be real. I went inside. Ceilings fans made slow shadows turn on broad white floorboards. Two of the walls were exposed brick floor to ceiling, decorated with posters featuring criminals wanted dead or alive, all tastefully framed as if they should have been hanging for sale in a gallery. The refrigerator in the back of the building seemed to be working, stocked with eggs, bacon, bread, and other breakfast foods. The grill was working too, and soon I was standing with a spatula while eggs and bacon popped and snapped and bread got brown in the toaster. The morning light was refracted by the dust and cobwebs in the windows. The cold wind blew the door open and closed. I'd never had a better breakfast. It was so good that when I was done I got up and cooked another one, and another one after that, amazed that I didn't feel bloated.

I heard music playing softly from a room above the café. I found a small staircase in a hallway in back of the kitchen. My dog ran ahead of me up the stairs, then started barking furiously in the room above. I entered the room prepared to make an apology. But except for my dog barking at the wind in the drapes, there seemed to be no one there. From a CD player on a nightstand by a bed, I heard the same music I'd heard the past few nights. I had to admit that the DJ was right: the music sounded like jazz being played on the moon, where the sounds were free to perform in ways that the fierce gravitational pull of the earth prevented or confined, a composition designed for the absence of an atmosphere, taking the place of an atmosphere. I tried to make my dog sit, but he started barking again and ran out the door. I got up and followed him down the stairs, through the café, and into the street. It was already dark. A half moon lit the mountains in the west. The music from the second floor window stopped and the light went out.

I got back in my car and drove down the mountain. The moonlight made the driving fast and easy. I reached the desert floor an hour before dawn. I stopped for gas. Finally the convenience store was open. The girl at the counter was tall and dressed in a white sweatshirt. If she'd had glasses, she would have been the waitress in the café. She looked at me as if she'd never seen me before, and I knew that if she were really the same young woman, she would have recognized me. But then it occurred to me that without her glasses, she couldn't see me clearly.

I said: Hi there. Do you have any maps?

She said: Maps? What kind of maps are you looking for?

I said: Maps of the region. A simple road map will be fine. Do you have one?

She said: Let me check.

She went back into a small room furnished with a gray metal desk and a row of metal file cabinets. I heard her open a drawer. I heard her mumbling to herself. Her voice became a voice in my head, the voice of an old friend in a phone conversation a week before, when he called to say that he'd finally gotten a cell phone. After struggling to make out his words mangled by satellite transmission, I asked him to call me back on a real phone.

He said: This *is* a real phone, and right now I'm on my way to the bank. I'm talking to you from my car. It's the first time I've ever driven and talked on the phone at the same time. I used to think it was dangerous when other people did it. But now that I'm doing it myself, it really feels cool.

I laughed: I can't believe what I'm hearing. After all the times we ridiculed people for getting caught up in hi-tech fads, here you are, caught up in a hi-tech fad.

He said: Right. But now that I've got a cell, I can't imagine living without one. I mean, I can get in touch with anyone from anywhere at any time.

I said: Yeah, but *they* can get in touch with *you* whenever *they* want to. You're a moving target.

He laughed: When people get in touch with you, you feel like a target?

I said: I just think it's important to have chunks of time when I'm not hooked up to the rest of the world.

He said: Sounds to me like you'd like *huge* chunks of time when you're not hooked up to the rest of the world. Why such a need to be out of touch? I mean, I haven't heard from you in months.

I said: I'm always dealing with people at my job.

When I'm not at work, I need time to myself. I—

He cut me off with something I wasn't prepared for: You know what? I've been thinking about the way you keep to yourself all the time. And it seems to me you've got a Noble Victim Complex. I heard someone talking about it on TV the other night, and he was saying that—

I said: I've never thought of myself as a victim. It's just that I—

He said: It's just that you isolate yourself from what's happening in the world and then complain when you think you don't get what you deserve. But never mind, I'll change my wording. How about a Noble *Outcast* Complex?

I said: Actually, I think words like *outcast* are too extreme, too theatrical, at least when they're applied to people like me, who haven't really been cast out of anything. It's true that I'm easily annoyed and try to avoid things that annoy me or give me anxiety. But really, if you're not annoyed by all the idiots glowing with hi-tech happiness, it probably means you've become one of them—

He said: In other words, you're not just easily annoyed; you're also paranoid.

I said: I feel like the main character in *Invasion of the Body Snatchers*—not that asinine remake that came out during the Reagan years, but the '50s original, starring Kevin McCarthy—and I'm talking to someone who used to be my friend, except that now he's become a pod person, with headphones in his ears and—

I stopped because I could tell that at some point in the past five seconds, our connection had been broken, and before he could call me back I went outside and took a long walk. I saw people on cell phones everywhere, eyes bright in a trance of hi-tech happiness. I knew I had to get out.

The pain of that moment brought me back to the present. I looked around the store. Everything on the magazine rack was in black and white, as if I were back in the 1940s and cell phones, TVs, and computers didn't exist yet. But if I were back in the 1940s, I wouldn't exist yet either, so I turned my attention back to the girl in the office. I was suddenly afraid that she might pull out a cell phone, calling her boss to see if there were maps in the store. But then she was back at the counter saying she didn't have any maps.

I said: Where can I get one?

She said: I don't think you can find any maps around here. At least, *I've* never seen one. What would you do with a map in a place like this?

I looked at her in silence. I thought of telling her how pleased I was that Bush and the Republicans were gone, but I wasn't sure what her political feelings were, so I kept my mouth shut. The moment stretched out and curled up like a dog preparing to sleep. I told myself that if I could gently nudge it awake, it might open its eyes and playfully lick my face. I felt confident. I decided to try something bold. I said: By the way, my name's Phil.

I extended my hand. Of course, I hadn't given her my real name. But I wanted to see if using the name Phil would make her use the name Connie, confirming my belief that words were nothing in themselves, mere sounds in the air or marks on a page that became significant only in relation to each other.

She reached into the pockets of her apron, pulled out her glasses, put them on and blinked three times. Without shaking my hand, she leaned forward, narrowed her eyes, looked at me closely and said: Can I help you with anything else?

I wasn't sure what to say so I said: Do you have any dog food?

She said: For you or for your dog?

She burst out laughing. I started to laugh but something about it felt wrong, so I told her to have a nice day and got back on the road. I drove for several hours. The sun came up but before long it was setting. I wondered if the death of time meant that the world itself was ending. I didn't think so. But I did think that things were out of balance, that the human race had been abusing time for so long that time now existed only to give space the time it needed, and it seemed to be needing less and less, perhaps because it was now taking the two-dimensional form of a landscape photograph, framed as a decoration above a mantelpiece in a room in a world where the human race didn't exist. For maybe ten seconds I saw the photograph clearly. But the image became something else then something else then something else, as if it existed solely for the purpose of changing itself, dissolving when I came to an old hotel.

I stopped and went inside. The check-in clerk was snoring with his head in his arms on a dark wood counter. I quietly slipped a key off a hook and tiptoed up the stairs in the back of the lobby. The room was on the top floor, three flights up. It had a great view of the desert, the moon fading into the dawn above the silhouettes of mountains. I watched until the sun was almost up. Then I got in bed.

I've never liked hotel bedsheets. They always feel stiff and formal. But the sheets in this bed felt like I'd been using them all my life, which made the process of falling asleep so delicious that it seemed to be happening over and over again, the same dissolving image of a half moon in a window framing the silhouettes of mountains. Then suddenly I was awake six hours later, pleasantly rested and ready for breakfast. As I went downstairs I could smell bacon and eggs from the café beside the lobby. The place was charming, with brick walls, old wooden tables, and broad oak floorboards. Patterns of light and shade played in the folds of lace curtains tossing slightly in the breeze. Three men wearing dark robes and conic black hats were sitting in three corners of the room. I sat in the fourth corner, completing the pattern. The three men ate with such pleasure that I felt I was eating their meals, and after a few minutes I was so full and satisfied that I knew what I had to do.

First I would find a part-time job. Maybe they needed help at the desk in the lobby. Maybe they would offer me free room and board and a little spending money on the side. Next I would get to know as many local people as possible. Once I'd become well known in the town, I could serve on the town council and before too long become the mayor. Then I would get a law passed banning cell phones, turning the town and perhaps the whole county into cell phone-free zones— and ultimately into media-free zones. With any luck, I could even restore the missing fragments of time. It was true that I'd never been in politics. It was true that I had no appetite or aptitude for the kind of semi-human interaction politicians need to master. It was true that there might be state laws preventing local politicians from banning destructive technologies. It was true that the town might not exist anymore. But what choice did I have? Though I knew that cell phones would be obsolete within ten years, this would only mean that the phonies had been given something even dumber to waste their time with, that the nation had become even dumber than before.

I walked out into the lobby and woke the guy at the desk by touching his arm. His head shot back in alarm. He looked at me like I was crazy. For one long moment I thought he might have a gun, a badge, and handcuffs. But when I told him I wanted a job he nodded with obvious pleasure. He smiled as if he'd found his long-lost brother.

# FOOD

Stopping in the middle of a sentence, distracted by thoughts about food, he closes the book without marking his place, even though it's not time for a meal, even though the sentence was holding his interest, making the claim that mainstream reality doesn't exist anymore, that at this point we can only talk about mainstream unreality, an assertion that's not as simple as it sounds, not when the distinction between real and unreal has been relentlessly blurred by the mainstream itself, to such an extent that the mainstream exists only because real and unreal have become interchangeable terms, generating a confusion so pervasive that it hardly seems to exist, functioning as a background noise that you notice only when it's not there anymore, but such moments of silence are unusual, difficult to recognize and even more difficult to sustain, provisional in a way that makes you feel insecure, like you need more control, the power to make such moments happen at will, as if the creation of silence were a skill you could learn in a classroom, but when the lesson appears on a blackboard, and the words are as precise as any professor could possibly make them, there's something that won't fall into place, something that still makes trouble, something that even experts are confused by, experts like Professor Food, a man who's been teaching long enough to know what he's talking about, long enough to know that he doesn't know what he's talking about, standing in front of the classroom with a piece of chalk in his hand, saying things he's learned to say by saying them over and over again, things he didn't fully understand until he said them, as if unspoken words were like uninflated balloons, a figure of speech he enjoyed when he first came up with it, though he's not sure now if words and balloons can really be compared, but he keeps producing the words and the faces facing him keep writing them down, concerned that what they don't write down might work against them later, though some of them are distracted by what's outside, by colors and faces and words on walls of billboards moving closer, blocking out most of the view from the classroom windows, making the classroom clock seem larger and louder than it really is, magnified seconds made of magnified nanoseconds ticking away, or not ticking away but stretching out and curling back on themselves, serpents flicking their tongues and flashing their fangs and eating their tails, while underneath the clock a student wants to raise her hand, a blond math major wearing high heels, a lumberjack shirt and a baseball hat, an outfit that makes a statement by refusing to make a statement, making several statements at once that cancel each other out, and she's wondering why the billboards keep getting closer, wondering why the lesson is always the same, word by word and phrase by phrase not a syllable out of place, but she's not sure how smart it would be to say anything, since the first question would show that she's not focused on Professor Food's lecture, and the second question would imply that he's too lazy or too dumb to come up with anything new, even though Professor Food has already justified his teaching strategy, announcing on the first day of class that every class would consist of exactly the same lecture, word by word and phrase by phrase not a syllable out of place, since his goal was to make sure students *fully* understood the material, not just in their brains but in every cell of their bodies, and he claimed that this could only be done through repetition, as if the lecture were an elaborate mantra, hypnotically seeping through the conceptual

and emotional superstructure of the mind, slowly undo-
ing toxic patterns of thought and feeling locked into
place so firmly that nothing else seemed even remotely
possible, but of course there was really no question of
repetition, because the lecture on second hearing would
be different from the lecture on first hearing, different
the third time around than the second, different heard
for the fourth time than the third, different on the fifth
day of class than on the fourth, and besides, Professor
Food firmly believes that it's crucial for students to
learn to cope with annoyance, since so much of life is
annoying and you can either be pissed off most of the
time or you can preserve your sanity by mastering the
annoyances, in much the same way that a surfer masters
a wave, but the blond math major doesn't like surfing at
all, so instead of raising her hand she gets up and leaves,
just as Professor Food turns and writes the word black-
board on the blackboard and the students bend over
their desks and write the word notebook in their note-
books, everyone so focused that they don't know at first
that she's just gone out, but the sharp sound of her high
heels in the corridor gives her away, a sound so compel-
ling that after ten seconds it's hard to tell if she's
approaching or moving away, a confusion that builds as
the sound continues, reaching a point where advancing
and receding are about to become the same thing,
destroying one of the basic oppositions that time and

space depend on, threatening an even more primal con-
dition, the distinction between possible and impossible,
which means that too much is at stake, activating the
occult mechanisms of universal correction, which
instantly turn the blond math major 180 degrees, send-
ing her back down the corridor toward the classroom,
leaving Professor Food with no doubt that the sound is
getting larger and larger, haunting him with an image of
high heels punishing a floor tiled like a chessboard, a
design that's always made him nervous, not because it
reminds him that he's never been good at chess, not
because the game includes menacing metaphors like
checkmate and stalemate, but because the floor reminds
him of other floors with the same design, places where
bad things must have happened, though he's never been
able to say what they were, and he doesn't think it would
help him if he could, especially since he's never been
convinced that he needs any help, except that at times
apparently harmless sounds affect him more than they
should, especially when combined with aggressive illu-
mination, light with a purpose, like the light that's all but
replacing the afternoon sunlight in the windows, buzz-
ing fluorescent light from walls of billboards moving
closer, smiling faces clever phrases calculated colors,
counterpointing the sound of high heels coming closer
and closer, turning Professor Food toward the class-
room door, just as the blond math major sticks her head

back into the room, giggling nervously, trying to be
sheepishly cute and act like nothing is going on, which
loosely speaking might be true but strictly speaking
can't be true, since something is always going on, even
if it's on a scale too small for human perception, and
the difference between something going on and noth-
ing going on is on the verge of dissolving, threatening
yet another primordial condition—the distinction
between what is and what isn't—leading the blond math
major to sit back down beneath the classroom clock,
scribbling furiously in her notebook in response to Pro-
fessor Food's description of a blond math major scrib-
bling furiously in her notebook, not quite understand-
ing what she's writing, and she ends up mixing Profes-
sor Food's words with her own words, half transcrip-
tion half translation half misunderstanding, but three
halves don't make a whole, making instead an unstable
condition, like a table with a missing leg, like a story no
one seems to be telling, focusing on a prominent quan-
tum physicist, a woman whose parents got rich by writ-
ing advertising jingles, money that's helped her move to
a place where jingles don't exist, a huge Victorian house
on the western shores of Lake Baikal in Siberia, and
she's used her family fortune to build an amazing device,
something that looks like a pile of junk but allows her
to reduce herself to the size of subatomic particles,
things with weird names that exist for less than a

millionth of a second, but a millionth of a second seems to take decades when she finally makes herself small enough to look the subatomic realm in the face, an image that she thought was only a metaphor when she wrote it in a recent journal article, but now that she's there it all appears to be just like what she left behind, people in houses waking up and eating and talking and laughing, trees bending in the breeze, jazz in low-lit basement clubs, aisles of food in labeled cans and bags, rattlesnakes making figure eights in desert sand, mystical dancers making figure eights in desert sand, planes that look like hammerhead sharks dropping bombs on a Third World country, people in observation balloons delighted by panoramas, drivers on freeways getting pissed off and giving each other the finger, out of work middle-aged men forced to take jobs delivering pizza, café conversations in which people keep changing the subject, but she tells herself that it's all so small that no one else even knows it's there, and when her device brings her back to the top-floor lab in her Siberian house, windows facing miles and miles of the deepest lake in the world, she can't quite bring herself to begin a scientific paper, knowing that she'd be laughed off the face of the earth if she wrote what she knows, but over time the frustration of having to keep quiet about a momentous discovery drives her to contact an old college friend, an avant-garde filmmaker whose parents died in a famous ballooning disaster, and through an eager exchange of emails they plan to make a documentary film about the sub-atomic world, protecting themselves from the scorn of the scientific world by framing the film as a work of fiction, but fights over details jeopardize the project, and one late afternoon, after a vicious disagreement about quarks and leptons, the filmmaker feels like someone trapped in a prepositional phrase about food, the very same phrase that appears in Professor Food's lecture, scribbled into the notebook of an attentive young man in the front row, an astrology major with short black hair and a long white beard and a varsity sweater, someone who would surely be every teacher's dream if he weren't listening so aggressively, changing what he's listening to, transforming a detailed discussion of symbolism in ice cream commercials into a detailed discussion of movie trailers, the way would-be actors and actresses avoid waiting on tables by making stupid movies sound brilliant, thrilling, profound, stunning, breathtaking, cultivating a seductive and authoritative manner of speaking, showing that even the most vacant nonsense can sound impressive if the speaker knows how to use her voice, something that has disturbing political implications that need careful attention, except that now the astrology major is transforming Professor Food's remarks on the need to protect animals from human violence, the need for an ongoing critique of humanity's master species complex, into a playful description of puppies in cardboard boxes, offered in shopping malls throughout the nation, bringing love into thousands of homes that would otherwise be dominated by Republicans or born-again Christians convinced that rhetoric about national security or family values is more than just the latest official installment of toxic nonsense, more than just an indication of how brain-dead the USA has become in the past thirty years, though it's foolish to assume that the USA has ever been smarter than it is now, and perhaps a more accurate way to approach the problem is to focus on what happens when a military superpower becomes obsessed with amusing and ornamenting itself with hi-tech devices like the cell phone that won't stop ring-toning in the astrology major's pocket, the kind of intrusion that used to make everyone giggle, but it's become so commonplace that no one notices, least of all Professor Food, whose discussion of substitute gratifications appears in the astrology major's notebook as a team of mountain climbers returning from a remote summit speaking a language no one has ever heard before, an image that affects the astrology major so physically that he feels like he's walking down an urban street on a chilly day at half past noon, a sidewalk of squares that keep repeating themselves, exactly the same size and shade of grey, and he's gotten to the point where he doesn't know how long he's been walking, except that he knows he's moving south, south becoming deeper south becoming deeper and deeper south, reaching a sky-blue boundary beyond which motion is no longer possible, the place where the sky comes down to meet the pavement, something that he's always thought was an optical illusion, or perhaps an optical metaphor, but now he walks face-first into what feels like blue plate glass, and there's nothing to do but turn and walk in the opposite direction, a sidewalk of identical squares repeating themselves, a trance of motion making the north appear to recede forever, except that he's suddenly face to face with a plate-glass boundary again, a blue so flat it's clear that on the other side motion doesn't exist, a firm indication that north and south aren't what they were before, so he tries walking east and bangs his face against the same blue boundary, and he tries walking west and the squares of the sidewalk end at the same blue boundary, forcing him to conclude that profound changes have taken place undetected, that the open transparent space he used to take for granted has been severely compromised, but instead of just waiting there at that suddenly rigid boundary, fondling his crotch or picking his nose, the astrology major slips quietly out of the classroom as soon as Professor Food turns to write something about mountains and language on the blackboard, chalk scraping across the flat black surface with the sound of skates on ice, a sound that follows the astrology major down the corridor, past paintings of smiling men and women who gave the school money, all posing with the same mountain meadow in the background, beyond which in the corner of his eye the astrology major expects to see a blue observation balloon, bobbing pleasantly between clouds that look like brains, reminding him of a trip he once took through mountains and meadows, taking shelter from a sudden storm in a cottage empty except for three unlabeled cans of food, waiting out the storm for days, becoming so desperately hungry that he smashed open one of the cans and ate what looked like a human brain, smashed open a second can and ate what looked like a human heart, smashed open the final can and found himself inside the can looking out, but the memory collapses into the light at the end of the corridor, imagery on walls of billboards waiting outside the doors of the school, quickly convincing the astrology major that there's no point in leaving the building, that at least the classroom is still a media-free zone, an assumption that crumbles when he slips back into his seat and Professor Food's lecture becomes a commercial, flashed on a screen descending from the ceiling, separating Professor Food from the blackboard, apparently triggered by an outside source beyond Professor Food's control, an ad that begins with the sounds of battle, Custer with bullets and arrows whizzing past him, surrounded by Sioux and Cheyenne braves and hundreds of dying soldiers and horses, and a voice-over says YOU CAN'T ALWAYS RUN AWAY FROM YOUR PROBLEMS, as Custer looks to the sky and sees three flying saucers cutting through the blinding sunlight, suddenly becoming Tylenol tablets, and the voice-over says BUT YOU CAN FEEL BETTER ABOUT WHAT YOU CAN'T ESCAPE, and the tablets fill the sky with the sound of many rivers, spinning down one by one into Custer's mouth, just as an arrow goes in one ear and out the other, and the general falls with a smile on his face, the camera zooming in on his teeth, which gleam like symbols of eternal happiness, entering the astrology major's notebook as a harsh condemnation of a right-wing think tank, the Project for the New American Century, the un-elected group that secretly governs the nation, people the astrology major has never heard of, and he puts his hand up wanting to know more about them, but Professor Food calls on a finance major who's always making excuses for cutting class, a bald young man whose eyes suggest that he's permanently baffled, frustrated because he can't find the right medication, looking especially troubled now because the wall of billboards advancing in the windows reminds him of a Shakespeare play, something about a king who talks to witches, and the finance major can't recall if it's *Hamlet* or *Othello*, but he clearly recalls that woods were approaching a mad king's castle, and he also remembers the mad king's wife, pushing him to kill his way to the top, and the finance major wonders if Professor Food has such a wife at home, someone who talks in her sleep revealing her husband's murders, but the thought of Professor Food killing people is so absurd that the finance major comes within seconds of howling with laughter, stopping himself only by writing in his notebook that he knows he's inventing Professor Food, that he's always inventing Professor Food, assuming all sorts of things about his private life, assuming that he'd rather lecture than have a conversation, that he likes gazebos better than discos, that he hates politicians and thinks that voting is meaningless, that he doesn't take any drugs but uses popcorn as a drug, that he thinks world leaders who declare war should be on the front lines fighting, that he prefers puppies to children because puppies don't grow up to become people the way children do, that he wishes he could see just one cloud that didn't look like a picture of a cloud, that he dreams of living in a sparsely furnished hut on the coast of Norway, that he got mad when George Bush was allowed to leave the White House without being tried for crimes against humanity, that he likes frozen sunsets filled with the silhouettes of factory smokestacks, that he thinks the beach would be fine if there were no people there making noise, that his first wife didn't believe in ghosts and his second wife did, that he thinks people who kill animals for the fun of it should get the electric chair, that his current wife wears high heels during sex because it makes her feel taller, and the list of assumptions might keep getting longer, as if it existed only to keep getting longer, but the finance major can see Professor Food watching him, reading his thoughts, a phrase which reminds him of Professor Food's claim that all reading is misreading, that the best we can do is accept that we're misreading everything, a claim that pissed off the finance major when Professor Food emphasized it in his opening lecture a few weeks before, but now the finance major finds it comforting, since it means that mind readers like Professor Food will always be wrong, reading their own concerns and tendencies into what they think they know, never seeing beyond themselves, but the comfort fades when the finance major begins to misread his own thoughts, begins to assume that he's always misreading his thoughts, an absurdity that's upsetting at first, but soon begins to seem funny, and this time he can only shut down his laughter by leaving the classroom, rushing to the drinking fountain, only to find that it doesn't work, so he staggers into the men's room and tries to drink from the sink, only to find that it doesn't work, so he turns and drinks from the toilet, drowning his laughter, giving himself the hiccups, and he feels like he needs fresh air, but when he stumbles down the corridor hoping his hiccups aren't loud enough to get him in trouble, he sees that there's no way out, that the billboards are coming closer, that the smiling teeth in the ads are getting sharper by the second, so he goes back into the bathroom and drinks from the toilet again, drowning his hiccups, then walks back into the class like nothing has happened, just as Professor Food says that nothing has happened, but the claim that nothing has happened apparently makes a great deal happen, music suddenly playing from hidden speakers in the ceiling, big hit songs that sound like ads that sound like big hit songs, all of them playing at once to become one song, lyrics that fasten themselves to the mind like parasites, seeming at first to be about boxes of laundry detergent left on the moon, then about weeds pushing up through cracks in abandoned swimming pools, then about windows made of hamburger meat, then about dusty globes in libraries closed because of budget cuts, then about ancient ruins that serve as landing sites for lightning bolts, and Professor Food swats at the music as if he were swatting at flies on a hot summer day, snarling and foaming at the mouth and cursing wildly, making up a whole new set of profanities, replacing words so badly overused that they've lost their offensive power, words like fuck and dick and shit and cunt, but his obscene anger only makes the music louder, driving him to grab two books from his desk to cover his ears, and the words in the books are used well enough to absorb the invasive sound, though once the room is quiet again the binding snaps and the pages crumble, making two heaps of dust on the floor, a very sad sight for a lover of books like Professor Food, but he doesn't have time to think about what's just happened, not when he sees that the finance major is just about to raise his hand, probably with a question that won't have much to do with the subject at hand, like the time he wanted to know the name of the Shakespeare play with the witches, even though at the time they were discussing the Bay of Pigs, so Professor Food calls on the smartest girl in the class, a chemistry major who wears exactly the same thing every day, torn jeans and a t-shirt that features a map of Alabama, and everyone hates the way she's always got her hand up, answering questions so brilliantly that no one remembers the questions, dominating the classroom with her voice, making everyone feel inferior, Professor Food included, except he knows that no matter how forceful her ideas are, he could easily put her in her place by exposing the true reasons for most of her opinions, her recent claim, for instance, that Anchorage and not Juneau should be the capital of Alaska, since Anchorage is a larger, more centrally located city, which sounded like flawless logic to the rest of the class, especially since her voice was calm and confident, but Professor Food could have pointed out that the chemistry major grew up in Juneau and hates it, has always thought of Anchorage as an escape, but not a total escape, since Anchorage is still in Alaska, still a symbolic extension of her nuclear family, revealing her inability to separate from her parents, something she tries to disguise by always wearing an Alabama t-shirt, connecting herself with a hot and humid state that's worlds apart from the frozen wastes of Alaska, but Professor Food can see through the deception, which is evident in the way the two states are spelled, since Alabama begins and ends with an A like Alaska does, another sign that she can't psychologically separate from her parents, a dirty secret that once exposed would threaten the credibility of everything she says, but Professor Food knows that he himself has dirty secrets informing his decisions about what to teach and how to teach it, and he's pretty sure that the chemistry major can see beyond his pedagogical surface, that she wouldn't hesitate to make him look silly if he tried to cut her down to size, so he does little more than nod and smile when she talks in class, even though he knows that he's tacitly affirming distorted information, which doesn't disturb him as much as other people might think it should, since he believes that all information is distorted, serving the needs and interests of those who call it information, a term which insists on its own authority, its right to be right, an attitude which Professor Food is eager to place on the right wing of the political spectrum, though he knows that lefties can also be dogmatic, and some of his best left-wing friends are self-righteous people, and in his stronger moments he's willing to admit that many people would describe him in the same way, but he tells himself that you have to stand for something, even if what you're standing for is your belief that all beliefs are nothing more than patterns of syllables, a point that Professor Food frequently makes when the chemistry major gets cocky, but this time she's chewing bubble gum, blowing a gigantic bubble, popping it, yawning and looking outside, recalling what she used to enjoy looking at, beyond the wall of billboards getting close enough to spit on, beyond the campus's old stone buildings covered with ivy, beyond the quaint college town, its well-preserved nineteenth-century houses, beyond the abandoned factory district on the edge of town, the jumble of blackened buildings and obsolete smokestacks, beyond the motels beside the freeway, beyond anything that the word beyond might mean to her, finally deciding that Professor Food's reduction of all knowledge to a pattern of syllables is in itself just another pattern of syllables, and she narrows her eyes and licks her lips and prepares to raise her hand, but suddenly there's laughter, not the aggressively defensive laughter of students who think they're way too cool to be thinking about Professor Food's ideas, not the secretive laughter of students passing notes or texting about things that have nothing to do with the class, but the high-pitched cackling that comes with evil experiments in dungeon laboratories, maniacal scientists in long black robes surrounded by steaming vats and bubbling alembics, a sound that bothers her because it seems to have come from nowhere, because it doesn't look like anyone in the classroom is laughing, and also because it seems to have come from a deep understanding of the lesson, something she's apparently unaware of, and she can't stand it when other people catch on faster than she does, leading her to think that maybe she's better off dropping the class, so she gets up and walks out in the middle of a sentence about alchemy in the Middle Ages, missing what Professor Food regards as the centerpiece of his discussion, the claim that the physical universe is a language words can directly affect, not so much because they allow us to construct plans that bring about actions and changes, but more because of their musical powers, the incantatory play of images riding on syllables, transforming the harmonic vibrations at the core of subatomic space-time, even if the term *core* is wrong, suggesting a solid center, when current speculation suggests that in the subatomic realm terms like solid and center have no meaning, and even though the chemistry major is beyond the range of Professor Food's voice by the time he starts talking about space-time, she knows all the words by heart, and all of her objections to the words by heart, the primary objection being that she doesn't think Professor Food has any business lecturing about something outside his field, though she found it intriguing at first when Professor Food began each class by denouncing specialization, claiming that it produced arrogant, narrow-minded people trapped in disciplinary ghettos, but after hearing the same argument so many times she's begun to think that Professor Food is only trashing specialized expertise because he's insecure about his own expertise, because he can't quite master the subject he claims to know best, so instead he's mastered ways of changing the subject, secretly making it something it's not, an academic sleight of hand that's no longer fooling the chemistry major, and she thinks it might be fun to play with Professor Food's insecurities, but now she's passing a room where a bald man wearing a blazer is giving advice to a long-haired student wearing a blazer, a young man gripping the sides of his chair, nodding eagerly whenever the advisor pauses, a situation that normally wouldn't hold the chemistry major's interest for more than a second, but there's a photo-realist painting of a moonlit cactus above the advisor's desk, and there's a large aquarium filled with tropical fish on a small gray file cabinet, and three feet away from the student's battered sandals there's a chocolate milkshake spilled on blood-red carpeting, and a ceiling fan is turning lethargically throwing shadows across the advisor's desk, throwing shadows across closed Venetian blinds, throwing shadows across a white wooden bookcase empty except for an old black boot on the bottom shelf, and the pattern of shapes and colors and motions holds the chemistry major in place for fifteen seconds, and each of those fifteen seconds feels like fifteen minutes, and each of those fifteen minutes feels like fifteen hours, and each of those fifteen hours feels like fifteen days, but near the end of the fifteenth day the chemistry major farts, breaking the spell, and she finds herself moving forcefully toward the door at the end of the corridor, a rectangle of harsh illumination that hurts her eyes, thousands of fluorescent lights throbbing above towering walls of billboards, ads for anything and everything blocking out the college town she used to see through the window in class, not just blocking it out but replacing it, or at least that's the claim that several billboards make, ads for cell phones featuring people whose eager expressions suggest that making mobile small talk is all that matters, and the chemistry major is the only student on campus who hasn't jailed herself in a cell phone yet, another reason Professor Food respects her even though he doesn't always like her, but now she's up against more than she can handle, staggering away from the harsh blasts of light in the doorway, rushing down the hall and down the stairs to the fire exit, but only getting the door half open before the blasts of billboard light force her to slam the door shut, leaving her with no voice, not even a voice to talk to herself with, though other voices talk in her head, urging her to buy herself back from whatever she can't afford, and she staggers back into the classroom knowing she smells like someone who's dumber than she was a few minutes ago, one of the few times in her life that she's been aware of feeling anything like mental insecurity, though the feeling is quickly replaced by astonishment, the realization that something is radically different in the classroom, that Professor Food's lecture has taken an unforeseen path, and he's claiming that human beings have no moral right to exist anymore, that whatever people have done to each other for the past ten thousand years, it's nothing compared to what they've done to the rest of the planet, which means that the only responsible action at this point is for the human race to destroy itself, a claim that the chemistry major would normally find absurd, but in the present situation the claim itself doesn't seem nearly as important as the fact that Professor Food has stopped repeating himself, a change that she can't account for since it happened when she was out of the class, a gap in her understanding that makes her feel even more insecure than before, adding to her fear that she probably looks like someone missing an obvious joke, that all her classmates can see how stupid she looks and feels, but no one even notices that she's back, their eyes drawn instead to what Professor Food has drawn on the blackboard, something that might be a magical diagram, a woodcut from a medieval book of spells, a sign that conjures fires of purification through destruction, though Professor Food himself doesn't know what he's doing, only what his hand has done with a piece of chalk on the blackboard, an image drawn with artistic skill far beyond what he's normally capable of, a picture of himself drawing a picture of himself drawing a picture of himself drawing a picture of himself, smaller and smaller scales of representation, culminating in a picture of a blackboard that's really a mirror sketched in so carefully that it mirrors all the scales of representation, forcing Professor Food to face his own face in a distant reflection, and behind his face he can almost see the mirrored student faces facing the blackboard, as if he were nothing more than a talking mirror, getting consumed in the endless play of reflections, digested by what the students think he's teaching them, digested by what he knows he's not really teaching them, and the gap that forms between what they think and what he knows gets hot, gets impossibly hot, more than impossibly hot, and it can't contain itself, flashing into quickly spreading fires that burn down the classroom, burn down the walls of billboards crushing the classroom on every side, quickly spreading all over the school getting hotter by the second, flames that sound like applause, flames that pause to enjoy what they're doing, flames that leap and dance, composing a shadow play on the flat white sky, flames that seem comprised of all of history's conflagrations—Rome Chicago San Francisco Dresden Hiroshima—flames with no connection to firebirds rising from their ashes, wildly approaching what might have been there before, the college town, its tidy rows of nineteenth-century houses, the abandoned factory district, blackened buildings and obsolete smokestacks, motels with their neon signs by the freeway flashing their vacancy, as if there would soon be nothing left but the vacancy, nothing to reduce to print and pictures, nothing to cut and paste and frame and sell, only a sentence twisting and turning away from where it began, making and remaking itself through changes in speed and focus, a tale that's eating its tail, a tale untelling itself in the telling, feeding on the eyes of someone feeding on what he thinks it means, someone getting distracted and turning away from the page to find food.

# REFUSAL AS RADICAL ACTION

I woke up hungry, more than hungry. I had a big breakfast and wanted more. I made myself a snack and wolfed it down and wanted more. I made myself another snack and still I wanted more. I wanted red meat, but I don't keep any red meat in the house. I swore it off a year ago, after reading a book about cows and pigs in slaughterhouses. I reminded myself that any red meat I bought would contribute to the gruesome things that the book described in such painful detail. I still felt hungry. I reminded myself that red meat gave me headaches and heartburn, made me feel sluggish and stupid and fat. I still felt hungry. When I sat at my desk and tried to get things done, the hunger just got worse.

When I got up and fed my dogs, I briefly thought about eating dog food.

Now it's time for lunch. I've decided to take myself out for a healthy meal. I step out into a typical San Diego sunny day, walking down a block that's filled with tanned and smiling people. I'm thinking they'd be disgusted if they knew I wanted red meat. They all look so oppressively undisturbed, so aggressively healthy. When I get to the corner and wait for the light to change, I start to feel relief. There's a vegetarian restaurant right across the street. I've eaten there many times and I like the food, though none of it ever triggers the kind of craving I've felt all morning. A tall blond woman taps me on the shoulder. She's looking at me like I should know who she is, like we're in the middle of a conversation and it's my turn to say something. I open my mouth to speak but nothing comes out. She smiles with all her teeth and says: Don't forget. Then she walks out into the street against the light and gets hit by a car.

For a second I feel nothing. Then less than nothing. Then a lot less than nothing. A guy beside me pulls out his cell and calls the appropriate people, but it's clear she's dead before the authorities come and make it official. Her blood, brains, and body parts are smeared all over the road. I want to cross the street and have lunch but I can't. I feel sick. I need to go home and think about what just happened. Why was a woman I'd never seen before telling me not to forget? Forget what? That she just told me not to forget? That her teeth were perfect? That she just got hit by a car? That I'm hungry? That I was born in Chicago? That it never snows in San Diego? That waterboarding has nothing to do with the beach? That things aren't what they used to be and they never were?

I get about halfway home before throwing up on someone's lawn. Fortunately, there's a drinking fountain across the street in the park, and I rinse out my mouth and splash water on my face. For a minute the very thought of food is repulsive. But my stomach feels empty, and my craving for meat returns, a cheeseburger with crisp and greasy French fries and a Coke. I tell myself again that such food is wrong, that I need to go home and try to calm down. But my feet are in charge, leading me toward the best greasy spoon in the city. I can already see the neon sign, GREAT! BURGERS. I've never been so hungry before. It's like I'm under a spell.

Sirens approach from several directions. I assume that they're coming because of what just happened on the corner, but soon it's clear that they're also responding to something else. People are stumbling out of GREAT! BURGERS, vomiting on the sidewalk. Across the street at McDonald's the same thing is happening.

Down the block, people stagger out from Wendy's, Denny's, and Burger King, doubled over, puking violently. I'm tempted to think that the meat they've eaten is making them sick, that in the future people who eat animals will be afflicted with terminal indigestion, driven mad by a nameless god capable of imposing mortal punishments, even if he doesn't exist.

But this wouldn't explain my own indigestion. It's been a year since I ate red meat, though I've heard that by divine standards wanting something is just as bad as doing it, or eating it, and certainly this morning I would have made myself at least one gigantic hamburger if I'd had ground beef in the house. People keep reeling out of the junk-food places puking their guts out, collapsing on the pavement, gripping their stomachs, gagging and moaning. An ambulance arrives, then a second one, then police cars. The street is filled with flashing lights, and I hear more sirens approaching, and other sirens far off in the distance, as if there were tragedy everywhere in the city. Has all the red meat in San Diego been poisoned? Or has there been a major shift in universal conditions, making it impossible to eat red meat anymore? I've got to get home and get some news from the radio.

When I rush through the door my two black labs look at me like I'm crazy, like I might start eating their food instead of feeding them. They look even more suspicious when I turn on the radio. They're sniffing the air and cocking their heads and searching my eyes for an answer. I almost never listen to the radio. I'm not sure why I haven't thrown it away, or why I got it in the first place. I don't like media noise, especially not in the house, and I don't think it's right to pollute my dogs' environment with the sound of mass information. But right now I don't care. I've got to find out what's going on.

The airwaves are filled with reports of worldwide vomiting, all of it near fast-food restaurants, burger joints, and steak houses. It sounds like the worst case of food poisoning in history, and I hear several experts say that normally they would suspect a terrorist plot, except that the situation seems to be connected to something that can't be so conveniently explained, reports that people all over the world are seeing things in the sky, not unidentified flying objects, but identified frying objects, gigantic versions of menu items: double cheeseburgers with onions and tomatoes, steak sandwiches with cheese, eggs and bacon popping and snapping in a skillet, Rueben sandwiches, buckets of Kentucky Fried Chicken, meatball sandwiches with marinara sauce, pork burritos, ham and Swiss cheese omelets, hot dogs covered with sauerkraut and mustard.

The mere mention of these foods makes me want to go out and stuff myself, even if this means that I'll spend the rest of my life throwing up. I switch off the radio, grip my chair, close my eyes, and try to find a quiet place in my head. But there's only random noise—gum jingles, newscaster voices, lines from books and magazines, fragments of popular melodies, movie trailer voice-overs—blending with the smiling face of the woman who told me not to forget. I want to tell her I won't forget, but I know I forget things all the time, minor things and major things, even when I remember to write things down. Right now I'd rather forget the whole day. I'm exhausted with confusion. I wish I could call my therapist, but I haven't seen him in more than a year, and besides, I'm drifting off. I sleep the rest of the day and through the night in my chair without dreaming, waking up with sunlight having breakfast on my face.

My dogs jump up and wag their tails when they see I'm awake. They're hungry. I'm hungry. I go to the kitchen and serve each one two cans of gourmet dog food, then I make myself a huge breakfast, a spinach and feta cheese omelet with a stack of buttered rye toast. I see from the calendar nailed to the wall that today I'll be having lunch with my friend Craig. We'll be meeting at The Green World, a health food place where we often get together and talk for hours. Today it's going to be difficult. They don't serve red meat at The Green World. It's going to be hard not to sneak in a

meal at GREAT! BURGERS—even at the risk of puk-
ing my guts out—before meeting Craig and pretend-
ing I'm still hungry. But if yesterday is any indication,
I won't have to pretend. Eating even a huge amount
won't stop me from wanting more.

I spend the morning making my living, editing
technical articles online. Since I've been doing it for
years, I can almost always finish quickly, three hours
a day at the most. Then the rest of the day is mine.
But today it's going slowly. I keep wondering what I'm
not supposed to forget. I can't stop making snacks and
checking the news. The radio and the Internet make it
seem like nothing happened. There's just all the normal
stuff about celebrities, football games, and the fucked-
up economy. One local station issues warnings about
high velocity winds coming down from the mountains
east of San Diego. But there's nothing about food in
the sky, nothing about worldwide indigestion, though I
know I heard reports yesterday on the radio. A media
cover-up? It wouldn't be the first time that important
developments have disappeared without a trace. But I
can't see why the captains of mass information would
want to exclude such sensational material, especially
since food was involved, and everyone knows that food
imagery is often used to stimulate consumer appetites.
Maybe they're trying to keep the world under control,
prevent the kind of panic that leads to widespread

violence and chaos. But would a sky of cheeseburgers really be scary enough to freak people out?

I force myself to take a long detour on my way to The Green World. If I went there directly I'd have to walk down junk-food row: GREAT! BURGERS, McDonald's, Wendy's, Denny's, and Burger King. I don't want to see the evidence of what happened there yesterday, all the vomit that might still be on the street. Besides, I know the temptation would be too great, and after I've eaten junk I get mentally sluggish. I want to be alert while talking with Craig. It's no fun sounding stupid when you're with an intelligent person. My detour takes me through Balboa Park, extending my walk by more than thirty minutes. It's a beautiful place, filled with lush vegetation that's hard to find anywhere else in this desert city, and I'm enjoying the view. The wind is filling the trees with sound and motion, making everything look even more alive than it normally does. I pass by the famous San Diego Zoo, the most deluxe animal incarceration site in the world. Normally, I try to avoid it, but today I'm grateful that I'm not near something I can eat. After all, the animals in the zoo aren't being prepared for human consumption, at least not the kind that involves a knife and fork.

Soon I can see the Museum of Man, its tower in the style of a Spanish Colonial church. As I get closer, I hear shouting and chanting. I see women carrying signs, a rally protesting the museum's name. I tell myself that only in San Diego could you get away with a name like the Museum of Man, but then it occurs to me that the name would pass without comment in almost any American city, that there are only a few places where the verbal sexism would even be noticed. The museum's current exhibit is "The History of Torture," which reminds me of something I read in a magazine recently, the results of a national survey showing that many Americans think that nothing really happened at Abu Ghraib, that the whole thing was a hoax and the pictures were fake, that American leaders never would have sanctioned such disgusting things. I wonder how many Americans think that the prisoners got what they deserved, that a country run by Saddam Hussein deserved whatever happened.

One of the protesting women steps out of the picket line and hands me a pamphlet. I glance at it and say: I'm sure what you're doing here is important, but I've been reading all morning, and I've reached a point where I can't stand words anymore.

She says: You must have been reading the wrong words.

I say: I was reading words that pay my rent.

She smiles: Like I said, you must have been reading the wrong words. The right words would've made you want to read more.

I'm not sure if she's trying to be funny, or trying to be serious by saying something funny, or trying to be funny by saying something serious, or just trying to be serious. I look at her carefully, hoping to see where she's coming from. She's fairly tall and heavyset with short black hair and a gray sweatshirt with a picture of a double-edged axe. The axe makes me think she's being sincere, so I say: It's not always easy to find the right words. This morning I was looking for them in the papers, but I couldn't find anything.

She says: The papers aren't the place to find the right words.

I get nervous when I'm talking to people I don't know, and I often tell pointless lies, like the claim I just made that I've actually read the papers, when I got my news from other sources. I feel like a jerk when I twist the facts, even if it's a harmless fabrication, and I'm always convinced that the person I'm talking to knows I'm lying. My usual approach is to try to get through the conversation as quickly as possible without being rude. But I've been dying to talk to someone about what happened yesterday, and this might be a good opportunity, so I nod and say: Yesterday was a good example. When the sky was filled with food, there was nothing in the papers about it, nothing at all, even though I heard reports on the radio.

She laughs: I heard those reports too, and so did

some of my friends. We agreed that it had to be some kind of hoax.

I say: But it wasn't a hoax. I saw hundreds of people vomiting yesterday afternoon on junk-food row.

She tries to smile, but it doesn't come off at all. She says: There might have been people vomiting, but how could there be hamburgers in the sky? Or giant hot dogs? The reports had to be a joke, or maybe a short story read on the radio, like the time Orson Welles read *War of the Worlds* on the radio, and people thought that men from Mars were invading the earth.

I nod and return her attempted smile, but I can tell she thinks I'm stupid for believing what I heard on the news. I change the subject, a skill I've mastered over the years because I don't like tense situations. I've gotten so good at changing the subject that people rarely notice. I ask her what the axe on her sweatshirt means.

She points to the pamphlet: Read this and find out.

She hurries back to the picket line shaking her head, where another woman wearing a gray sweatshirt with an axe is yelling into a megaphone. It distorts her words so thoroughly that the only thing I can make out is her anger. I've got my own anger to deal with now, my anger at myself. Why did I talk about food in the sky when I didn't see food in the sky? Why did I let the mass media tell me what I saw?

I look at the pamphlet briefly. The thought of axes makes me think of Barack Obama, soon to become the first non-white U.S. President. I think about how unsafe he is in a racist country like ours. There has to be at least one right-wing group with plans to assassinate him. The thought of it makes me want to find out who they are and expose them, make sure that their trial and execution are televised. I'm not pleased that I'm filled with such violent thoughts, but I see nothing wrong with extreme measures when the things they confront are worse. In fact, I've wondered many times over the past few years why no one has had the guts to assassinate George Bush and the big shots in his rich Republican support system.

I brought this up with Craig a few years ago, soon after the 2004 presidential election, and he asked me why I wasn't ready to do it myself. I told him I wouldn't know the first thing about assassinating someone. If I even began to make assassination plans, I'd probably make a mistake so obvious that I'd get rounded up as a terrorist and sent to Guantanamo to be tortured. Craig told me that unless I was ready to do something myself, I had no right to say that someone else ought to do it. At the time I simply nodded in agreement. But now that I think of it, it's funny that Craig would be concerned with the difference between doing something and discussing it.

Twenty years ago, Craig was doing anthropological fieldwork on a little-known Philippine island. He'd done fieldwork before and knew what he was doing, but the more he tried to write up and publish his findings, the more he saw that his way of describing one of the few remaining Paleolithic tribes in the world had nothing to do with the way they would have described themselves, assuming they would have described themselves at all. Craig decided that simply by approaching these people as intellectual subject matter, he was distorting what they really were. Though he went on to publish a well-received book on this tribe, he knew there was something wrong with what he was doing.

He never did field work again. From that point on, his writing focused on writing, on the ways in which narratives of all kinds make the world look more like a story than it really is. Craig's claim in subsequent articles and books was that knowledge itself is an authoritarian system, a collection of observations, opinions, and suppositions disguised as factual pictures of the world, and the job of the anthropologist was not to keep feeding the system with new scraps of so-called information, but to challenge the system's fundamental assumptions, its verbal methods of constructing and authenticating itself.

Of course this caused a commotion among Craig's colleagues, but it also made his career, establishing him as an outlaw celebrity in academic circles. Suddenly all

fieldwork was suspect. All First World claims about so-
called Third World cultures were suspect. Craig's pic-
ture was everywhere. Anthropology departments all
over the nation wanted him. He finally took a position
that required no fieldwork and almost no teaching. He'd
essentially been hired to write books claiming that writ-
ing itself was a fascist project, valid only if the writer
waged war on his own medium.

I remember how pleased with himself he was.
After all, he was beating the system, getting praise and
money from people whose values he was attacking.
I was impressed with how he'd taken a risk and suc-
ceeded. But it wasn't just his daring I admired. I liked
the idea that human knowledge was nothing more than
a house of cards, that if I sometimes got frustrated
with the limits of what I knew, I could always feel bet-
ter by reminding myself that no one else knew anything
either. But I couldn't get past a basic contradiction: if
Craig could declare war on writing and thinking, how
could he trust his own writing and thinking? From what
enlightened point of view was he making his judgments,
when the very notion of an enlightened point of view
was being called into question? Wasn't Craig's critical
perspective, his enlightened point of view, just another
house of cards?

When I brought this up with Craig he laughed
and changed the subject. When I tried to return to the

subject he changed it again. When I told him he was changing the subject he laughed and changed it again. I would have been upset if someone accused me of changing the subject, but Craig didn't seem disturbed. He looked me in the eye and his teeth were flashing in the sunlight. Thinking back on it now, I wish I'd asked him why getting caught in evasive behavior didn't make him feel sneaky and stupid. But I rarely have the composure to say what I wish I'd said when I think of it later.

The wind is getting more intense. Normally I love the wind, especially since anything more than a lively breeze is rare in San Diego. But right now the wind feels difficult, like it's coming from several directions at once, making it hard to keep track of what I'm thinking. Something keeps changing the subject, words becoming other words without consulting me first. It's like I'm part of a story someone I don't know can't stop telling. My hunger isn't going away. When the woman at the museum mentioned hamburgers and hot dogs, I wanted to be on junk-food row, vomiting or not. Again I get that feeling that I might be under a spell. I'm glad that The Green World is now just a block away.

When I open the door to the restaurant, there's a tall blond waitress laughing at something a man with an apron apparently said. She puts on a serious face as soon as she sees me, as if laughter on the job were a crime.

The guy in the apron shrugs and goes into the kitchen. He looks like my former therapist, tall and lean with short white hair, but he seems to be one of the cooks.

His joke must have been good. The waitress can barely keep a straight face. She struggles to look professional by straightening out her white uniform. In the past, Green World servers didn't have uniforms. They wore whatever they wanted to wear, part of the casual image that the owners seemed to want. Maybe new people are running the place. I'm hoping the food is still good, though I'm also hoping it's not still good and I can get a greasy cheeseburger with French fries and a Coke.

The waitress tries to give me her best professional smile and says: "Hi, I'm Tammy and I'll be your server today!" I return the smile but I'm annoyed by the scripted introduction. It never would have happened before. Is someone trying to turn a good health-food place into a boring family restaurant? Everything else about the place looks the same as it did before: broad oak floorboards and big wooden booths that look like they might have been taken from a nineteenth-century tavern. But maybe these things will soon be gone, replaced with linoleum floors and plastic tables. It certainly wouldn't be the first time that new owners have ruined something good. I'm thinking that Craig and I might have to meet somewhere else in the future.

She seats me in a booth beside a window. It looks out on the Museum of Man, its tower rising above the trees in the park, piercing the sky.

I smile and say: Nice view.

She says: Sure, if you like phallic symbols.

I'm not sure how to respond. Why would a server talk like that to a customer she's never seen before, especially if the restaurant wants to change its image, to seem cheerfully bland and conventional? It occurs to me that Tammy isn't as dumb as I thought at first, that maybe she thinks the uniform and the server script are just as absurd as I do. She's deeply tanned and blond like many San Diego women, so I quickly assumed that she had to be an idiot, a beach girl who would grow up to marry a suit and take her kids to family restaurants. But now I'm thinking I've made an unfair assumption. Even if she does like the beach, that doesn't mean she's stupid. Maybe she's got a Ph.D. in psycholinguistics, and she's only working here because she can't find a job in her field, like so many people these days. Like me, in fact. I couldn't find a job in my field and ended up doing something else. It's not bad work, but it's not the job I dreamed of. Thirty years ago, I wanted to do what Craig has ended up doing, practicing the art of interpretation. But maybe it's just as well that I didn't. After all, my reading of Tammy was probably wrong, and wrong or not, it was based on at least one stereotype.

Tammy hands me a menu, puts a glass of water on the table, and says that she'll be back in a few minutes. I notice a copy of yesterday's *New York Times Book Review* on a nearby table, and I decide to page through it while waiting for Craig. Normally I wouldn't bother. I hate the stuffy style of *New York Times* reviews. But this time the lead article gets my attention. It's a bitter attack on a work of fiction set in Abu Ghraib. I was thinking that someone should write a book or make a movie about what happened there, especially since so many people don't remember. But this new book, by someone named Solomon Stein, has apparently taken significant liberties in reconstructing the situation.

Most outrageous, the reviewer claims, is the author's use of President Bush, who near the end gets kidnapped, facially altered, and thrown into the prison with his tongue cut out. For several weeks the President, along with many peaceful but imprisoned Iraqi citizens, is treated abusively by American soldiers. Someone even takes a shit on his face. The President has no way of telling them who he is. He tries repeatedly to communicate by writing with his fingers in the dirt of his prison cell floor, but the soldiers just laugh, since they can see that he doesn't look like George Bush. When the President finally dies, his mangled face and body are photographed by the people who abducted him. The pictures circulate widely through the media, a warning to future Presidents to think twice before waging war. No one is really sure it's Bush, since his face has been altered and sliced up, but the President has been missing for more than a month and no one else can explain what happened to him. The authorities finally accept the outrageous truth.

The crowning touch—the ultimate outrage according to *Times* reviewer David Stone—is that the people responsible aren't Islamic terrorists. They're U.S. anti-war activists who make no attempt to escape the authorities, announcing that they're eager to appear before the nation and explain their actions. In a series of TV appearances that get higher ratings than the Beatles' three appearances on the Ed Sullivan Show, they claim that what they've done should be aesthetically classified as conceptual art and legally classified as justifiable homicide. The book ends before we find out what happens to them. Stone concludes his review by urging everyone not to read the book, claiming that it serves roughly the same function as the fictional picture of Bush's mangled, shit-stained face.

It seems obvious to me that by trashing the book so ferociously, Stone is working against his own purposes. In effect, he's publicizing the book's anti-war message by denouncing it in such a visible place. I'd be surprised if the book didn't become a *New York Times* best seller. This leads me to suspect a hoax. Are

Solomon Stein and David Stone the same person? Are both just fake names used by someone clever enough to know that raging reviews often work in the author's favor? The names are connected in devious ways: Solomon was David's son in the Bible, while Stein and Stone are only one letter apart, and *Stein* is German for *stone*. I'm eager to read the book and see if Stein and Stone have more or less the same style. But I'm guessing it's already sold out. I'll have to ask Craig if he's heard of it or knows who really wrote it.

Just as I mention him in my head, Craig enters The Green World, short and stocky with short black hair and a long white beard, a slightly bemused expression on his face, as if he's telling you that the world is so messed up that you can't quite laugh and you can't quite cry, but a blank expression won't work either, since it would suggest that you don't really care, and Craig would never want anyone to think that he doesn't care. He nods and slightly smiles and shakes my hand, sits and sighs and looks at me with weary eyes. I sigh and look at him with weary eyes.

He says: You know that conference I said I was going to avoid? They called me at the last minute and offered me five thousand dollars to give the keynote address and serve as a moderator on two panel discussions. I need extra money this summer for a trip I'm planning, so I said okay. But I feel like a zombie now.

You know I hate being around the kind of people that go to conferences.

I'm suspicious. It would have taken more than five thousand dollars to get me to go to a professional conference. I say: The only time I ever went to a conference—it must have been ten years ago—it took me weeks to recover. So I—

He says: Why did you go?

I don't remember why I went, so I say: I thought I could make new connections and expand my freelance business. At the time I didn't think I had enough clients and—

He says: I told myself I'd never do it again. But there I was, wearing a name tag, eating little cubes of cheese off toothpicks, drinking wine from clear plastic cups.

I say: The time I went, everyone was using the word *interrogate*. Instead of saying that they were questioning, examining, or challenging something, they all kept saying that they were *interrogating* it. If I hear that word again I think I'll throw up.

He says: Then it's a good thing you didn't come with me. I heard that word at least a hundred times last week.

I say: I guess that's the last time you'll ever go to a conference.

He shrugs and looks at the menu.

I shrug and look at the menu, thinking about what I've ordered before that I liked. The design of the menu is new. The food is mostly what they had here before, but each dish is described in such a lavish way that it sounds like a joke. I want to laugh but I'm distracted. I'm trying to decide if Craig's display of aversion to the conference is a cover-up. It's the kind of thing I can see myself doing, trashing something I like because I can't admit that I like it. I glance at Craig as he studies the menu. Was it really such a nightmare for him to be in the spotlight around people in his field? Here in San Diego, recreation capital of the world, no one knows who Craig is. He's not a celebrity. But at the conference, Craig was no doubt viewed as a major player. People recognized his name when they saw it on the program, and people he'd never met knew him by sight from photographs they'd seen in professional journals. I'm sure he felt flattered that they wanted him for the keynote address, even as a last-minute substitute.

Tammy comes to take our order. She tells us what the specials are. She's got them memorized. Craig jokes about how good her memory is. She tells him that his beard looks fake. He laughs and takes if off, stuffing it into his pocket. I'm trying to figure out if I've ever seen Craig with a long white beard. It doesn't seem likely, since his hair has always been black and he's not going grey. Then why didn't it bother me when he first walked in? He looks at me carefully, maybe wondering about my reaction to his suddenly beardless face.

He says: What's wrong? You look angry.

I know I can't say what I'm thinking, so I say: It's just that my mind keeps wandering. I can't focus. I had all sorts of things I wanted to talk about before I got here, but now I can't remember what they were.

He says: Maybe you better start writing things down.

I say: I wish I could. But I can't remember to write things down. And even when I do, it's like the writing itself is changing the subject, as if the words had other places to be.

He finds this funny. Or at least he's got a big smile on his face. I don't want to talk about writing things down, so I put a big smile on my face. The two smiles cancel each other out, and the temperature drops about ten degrees, then quickly goes back up again.

Tammy starts to say that she remembers things because she can't afford to forget, that people would get mad if she didn't get their orders right, and she'd get lower tips. But people at a table across the room are waving at her like they want the check or something for dessert, so she nods and smiles in their direction, tells us she'll be right back and hurries away. I'm impressed that she can handle a job like this, with people always wanting her attention.

I look outside. The wind is even stronger than before, blowing leaves and branches down the street beside the park, knocking over a garbage can, whirling trash all over the Green World parking lot. Suddenly I remember. I show Craig *The New York Times* and ask: Have you heard about this new book, this novel based on Abu Ghraib?

The big smile is back on his face: There's only one thing to say about Abu Ghraib, and I've already said it.

Craig's arrogance can be obnoxious. But I'm used to it. I'd probably be the same way if I'd gotten the kind of attention he's gotten over the years. I say: You mean that op-ed piece you did for the *L.A. Times*? I don't remember it all that well.

He looks annoyed, but he tries to sound calm: Then let me remind you. I won't quote myself exactly, but the argument was that people were missing the point about Abu Ghraib. So many people claimed to be surprised when they saw the pictures. This tells you something sinister about the success of the American image machine, the spell it casts every day on the minds of the nation. Think about it: Bush knew he could claim that Abu Ghraib was nothing more than a few crazy people doing evil things. According to Bush, it had nothing to do with the war itself or his way of doing things. He knew most people would buy such nonsense, since they've always been told that when our

country wages war we don't get nasty. Our elected offi-
cials wage only virtuous wars, and they wage them only
in virtuous ways, unlike those demonic leaders in places
like Iraq, Iran, Afghanistan, and North Korea.

I say: You don't think Bush believed his own
bullshit?

Craig says: Not for a second.

I say: I think he's put himself under a spell with-
out knowing it. He's so trapped in self-deceptions that
he has no connection to anything outside the absurd
story that he can't stop telling himself.

Craig says: There's no way to know. Bush him-
self is just an image, a collection of pictures and sound
bites.

I want to insist that Bush is more than an image,
but I can't get past what I just said, that Bush is trapped
in a story that he can't stop telling himself. I thought the
same thing about myself ten minutes ago, except I told
myself that someone else was telling the story.

Tammy comes back and asks us what we're hav-
ing. Craig quickly looks at the menu and orders veg-
etarian lasagna. I decide to have the same thing, mainly
because it reminds me of normal lasagna, which often
has red meat. I briefly feel embarrassed, assuming that
Tammy now thinks that I don't know how to think
for myself, that I can't make simple decisions, that the
best I can do is imitate my friends. She narrows her

eyes and seems to be focusing just above the bridge of my nose. I tell myself that she's reading my mind. I've never believed that anyone really has telepathic powers, but maybe Tammy has something else, something she learned from her study of psycholinguistics, assuming that's what her major was, assuming she went to college at all. I try to give her a look that says I'm not that easy to read, that I'm the kind of book teachers put on their syllabus to get the lazy students to drop the class. She smiles with all her teeth, as if she wanted us to see that she doesn't have any cavities. She tells us our food will be ready in ten or fifteen minutes, then smiles at someone waving at her from a table across the room. I watch her try to seem pleased that people keep wanting her attention.

Before she goes, she gives me that strange look again, like she's reading my mind, and I'm convinced that she looks quite a bit like the woman who told me not to forget. I'm surprised I didn't see the resemblance at first. But when I try to picture the suicide woman, I can't recall her face. I feel like an idiot. After all, she told me not to forget, but the only thing I remember is her teeth. They were perfect and looked like Tammy's perfect teeth, or like my ex-wife's teeth.

She called me a few days ago, at half past three in the morning. She'd finally seen how much of a jerk her current husband was, and now she wanted me back. When I told her I was doing fine on my own, she got mad and threatened to put me under a spell. She'd learned the art of casting spells from the man she left me to marry, who owned and directed a school of magical studies in northern New Mexico. A mutual friend informed me that she'd gone insane for a while, convincing herself that a demon had given her supernatural powers. Her doctors finally found her the right medication, and before too long she was functioning like a normal human being again, except that she still believed that she could put people under spells.

When she made her threat, I laughed and told her I didn't believe in spells. But now I'm not so sure. I've never been so hungry before. It really does feel like I'm being controlled by something else, something that's pretending to be me, telling me what I think and want and what I should do about it. I want to ask Craig if he's ever thought that he might be under a spell, but I'm afraid to sound like a fool. Still, I've got to say something. I can tell he can tell there's a question I want to ask. So I quickly think of a substitute question, which comes out wrong, like I'm conducting an interrogation instead of just talking, and of course I hate the word interrogate, but I manage to say: So Craig, what were you doing yesterday? Were you outside at about half past noon?

He looks alarmed: No. Why?

I say: Strange things were happening.

Craig reaches for his beard, as if it were still on his chin. I feel like telling him that it's fine with me if he puts it back on. He says: So I've heard.

I say: I'm sure you heard about the vomiting on junk-food row. I was there. I saw it happen. But right before that, I was going for lunch at The Happy Earth, and I was standing on a corner when a woman tapped me on the shoulder and smiled and told me not to forget. Then she ran out into the street and got hit by a car. I was—

Craig puts his hand on the table as if it were a basketball that he was getting ready to slam-dunk. He says: Last week at the conference, I was eating lunch with Bruce Duncan—

I'm annoyed that he just changed the subject, but I say: Bruce Duncan? I thought you hated him.

Craig says: I do. But he wanted to talk to me about publishing my keynote address in his journal, and he volunteered to pay for my lunch. So we were sitting there eating when I looked at the salt and pepper shakers on the table, and they did a little dance, as if they were Fred Astaire and Ginger Rogers. It took about thirty seconds.

I say: With music? Did Bruce Duncan see it too?

Craig says: Yes and yes. The music was like something Fred Astaire and Ginger Rogers might have danced to, and Bruce definitely saw it, and we traded puzzled glances. But we were right in the middle of an intense conversation, and when I tried to mention it later one of his grad students came to the table and said she had to talk to him right away. He rushed off with her and I didn't see him again at the conference.

I notice that our table has no salt and pepper shakers. Looking around, I can't see any salt and pepper shakers on the tables. I guess The Green World doesn't believe in altering the tastes that Mother Nature gave her food. But if the place is on its way to becoming a family restaurant, it's sure to have salt and pepper on the tables before too long. The way I feel right now, I could dump a full box of salt on a juicy cheeseburger bigger than a turntable. The craving is so intense that I have to remind myself that turntables don't exist anymore, except in thrift shops.

Craig says: Has anything like that ever happened to you?

I decide that it's time to get back at him for changing the subject. Instead of answering his question, I tell him how stupid I felt when I told the feminist at the museum about the food I'd seen in the sky.

Craig looks puzzled: What made you feel so stupid?

I say: I didn't see food in the sky. I just heard about it on the radio. I fell for a hoax.

163

He gives me a puzzled look and says: Hoax? There was no hoax.

I say: You're telling me that the sky was really filled with cheeseburgers and fried eggs?

He smiles: And hot dogs covered with sauerkraut and mustard.

I say: You're not joking? You saw the food in the sky?

He says: I didn't actually see it, but my friend Priscilla did, and Priscilla doesn't make things up. It's not her style. In addition to being my friend, she's my accountant. The only time she lies is when she does my taxes.

I say: Where was she when she saw the food?

Craig says: In her office. She's got a big picture window facing the ocean.

At first she just thought the sky was filled with strange clouds. But when they came closer, she saw that she was looking at food—cheeseburgers, Rueben sandwiches, ham and Swiss cheese omelets. Of course she thought at first that something was wrong with her vision. But the other people in her building saw food in the sky too, and they were freaking out, running up and down the corridors, shouting and slamming doors. But Priscilla just sat at her desk and watched.

I say: Why would food in the sky freak people out? Sure, it's weird, you don't expect it. But I don't see why anyone would feel menaced.

Craig says: I think it has something to do with size. When you see a pork burrito the size of a football field, your brain can't take it in. Your body panics, even if you know there's no real threat.

I say: So what happened after everyone freaked out?

Craig says: Nothing happened. Priscilla sat there watching, and finally the food went away.

I say: And then she called you up and told you what happened?

Craig says: She told me when she came over last night, right after we finished making love.

I say: So Priscilla's your lover. You never told me.

Craig says: Right. And please don't tell anyone else. I don't want my colleagues to know that I'm sleeping with an accountant, especially since she's also a Republican.

In Craig's line of work, people who work with numbers are viewed with contempt. They're seen as uncreative hacks, doing work that a robot could do.

I say: My lips are sealed. But I still want to know what you think about that woman killing herself on the street yesterday. What do you think she meant by *Don't forget*?

He shrugs: There's no way to know. Don't forget that you watched her kill herself? Don't forget the important things in life? Don't forget to brush your

teeth? Don't forget about Abu Ghraib? Don't forget
who you are? Don't forget that you're not who you
think you are? There's no way to know.

Tammy comes back and says: Your food will be
here in a minute.

The mere mention of food makes me want to
rush into the kitchen and eat everything I can find. I'm
wondering why Tammy didn't start us off with a basket
of bread and butter. I don't want to look like I'm under
a spell, so I smile at her and tell her there's no hurry.

Craig says: As I just said, there's no way to know
for sure what *she* meant.

Tammy says: Who?

Craig ignores her and says: The important thing
is what *you* think she meant, what *you* think is impor-
tant about not forgetting. I made the case in a recent
essay that refusing to forget is a radical action, a way of
resisting the official amnesia produced by mainstream
culture.

He's quoting himself again, but this time it doesn't
bother me all that much because I agree with him. I'm
nodding along with every word.

Tammy says: Do you guys really think that any-
one's *actively trying* to make you forget?

Craig says: I—

I say: I—

But Tammy has already turned. She makes a beeline for the bathroom. Two first-person pronouns hang in vegetarian silence, in air that's never been tarnished by the smell of grilled and greasy red meat.

We look at each other wondering how to talk without first-person singular pronouns. First-person plural won't work. It makes you sound schizophrenic. *You* has more potential but still has limitations, a history of being marked wrong on high school compositions. We could try to talk without pronouns, like the prose in scholarly journals, but we've always agreed that scholarly journals are boring.

The cook steps out of the kitchen, glancing quickly around the room. Our eyes meet but it's like he doesn't see me. He still looks like a therapist I was seeing five years ago, a guy whose technique involved a book of ancient symbols, woodcuts on yellowed pages that looked old enough to crumble on contact but held together quite well when I actually turned them with my hand. Each symbol was an abstract pattern I'd never seen before. When I looked for more than thirty seconds, the symbol turned into something else I'd never seen before, and thirty seconds later became something else which became something else. The therapist told me to turn the page only when the symbol stopped changing, which sometimes happened in thirty seconds and sometimes in thirty minutes. Each session went the same way as we slowly worked our way through the book, which seemed to grow a new page with each page I turned. I felt like I was being changed, as if the transformation of shapes that meant nothing to me was changing the way I thought about things that did mean something to me. Parts of my life I'd forgotten were coming back to me, crucial recollections—things from childhood, things from high school and college, things from dreams. I was pleased with my progress. I'd never done such meaningful reading before.

But my therapist always reminded me that the book was just a first step, preparation for something else, the power to read images in the world and not just on the page, signs I would learn to recognize once I'd advanced my skills with the book. At the time I wasn't sure what he meant, but now it occurs to me that a cheeseburger in the sky might be one of those magical images, and it only seems absurd instead of magical because I'm not evolved enough to read it properly. Or maybe my confusion shows that I'm already reading quite well. Maybe confusion has gotten a bad rap over the years. Maybe it deserves more respect than it usually gets. This thought appeals to me greatly, but I know I might be kidding myself. I often do. Maybe confusion is no more than it seems: a mental mess. And how would all the vomiting fit in? Could someone barfing possibly be seen as a magical image? It seems too crude, but maybe it's my concept of magic that's crude. Maybe my mental images of magic are blocking me from seeing what magic really is. I wish I could call my therapist and discuss the situation. But he's not my therapist anymore. After nine months of the book, he said we had to stop, that he was broke and had to find a way to make more money. Has he gotten a job as a cook?

I look back at the cook but he's turned away. I keep looking. He doesn't look back. The men in the next booth are laughing loudly, pounding the table, talking about stolen identities. One of them claims that identities can't be stolen, that the motions concealed by the static shape of a first-person singular pronoun can't be held in place long enough to be taken away. A man with a shiny bald head makes a firm declaration, talking as if he wants everyone in the room to hear what he's saying: The *I* itself could be stolen, but not what it signifies.

The other four men at the table find this funny. They're laughing and pounding the table even harder than before. At first I'm tempted to laugh along with them, even though I'm not part of their group. The laughter shows no sign of letting up. It starts to feel sinister, as if they might really know how to steal identities, or at least the linguistic surfaces of identities. Maybe they're practicing some kind of evil magic. Maybe they're members of a secret society. I wonder if they have a book of spells.

Suddenly they're all silent, like junior high school students when the teacher unexpectedly walks back into the classroom. The moment waits for something to happen. Nothing does. The moment waits. It waits and waits and waits for something to happen. Nothing does. I decide that the moment must be waiting for me to change the subject, so I think about what I'll be doing later, when lunch is over. I decide that I'll get a bag of burgers to go from GREAT! BURGERS, then go home and check on YouTube to see if anyone has a video of the sky yesterday. People seem to be filming almost everything these days, as if they're always waiting with their cameras, as if the whole purpose of life is to get things on film. But what if what's on YouTube is fake? What if the whole thing yesterday was staged, and they used a computer to make images of a sky filled with greasy cheeseburgers, then put it on the Internet as a hoax? I know Craig said his Republican lover saw food in the sky, but I can't be sure that he isn't joking. He's played tricks like this on me before, and it's also hard to believe he would sleep with a Republican.

I look back at the cook but he's still turned away. I look back into the space of missing pronouns. I take a deep breath, pulling something into my mouth. It tastes like me. Craig sees what I'm doing and does the same thing. Earlier I imitated him. Now he's imitating me.

I say: That was pretty weird. I felt like my first-person singular sense of myself was floating about an inch in front of my face, like a small transparent balloon.

Craig says: That's what I felt too. Though to me it seemed like the first-person pronoun was the dripping of a leaky faucet somewhere behind my head.

I say: Do you think those guys at the next table had something to do with it?

Craig says: They sound pretty messed up. Maybe they work for an advertising firm or a TV station, and they're in the business of stealing people's identities. They want us to forget who we are so they can tell us who we are.

I say: Or maybe they're just the kind of New Age weirdos that tend to hang out in places like this.

Tammy comes from the bathroom talking on her cell phone. Again I catch myself thinking she's an idiot. I hate cell phones. Or rather I hate the way people get excited about them, raving about all the new things you can do if you buy the latest model. Craig and I are probably the only people in San Diego without cell phones. I knew one other guy who didn't have one, but he got so disgusted by the way people fetishize them that he disappeared into the desert with his dog.

Tammy talks into her phone: That's *always* how it was with us! Always always always! Like I was part of some story you couldn't stop telling. I—

Her body locks into place, a freeze frame in a movie. Her cell phone drops on the table with a bang. The guy on the other end keeps talking, though I can't make out the words. The voice sounds like a mosquito trapped in a can. Craig looks disturbed, worse than disturbed. He says: I've really got to get out of here. Ever since I got that mosquito bite in the Philippines, I've been terrified of mosquitoes.

I tell him it's not really a mosquito, but he gets up and says: It doesn't matter. The sound itself is enough to make me sick. I'll call you later.

When he goes outside the wind is so strong that he has to struggle to close the door. The wind slams it open again, and Craig has to work hard to close it a second time. I think back to his experience in the Philippines, the last place Craig did field work. Apparently the mosquito that bit him was dangerous. People had been known to die from its bites. Craig survived, but for more than a year he couldn't get an erection.

I pick up Tammy's phone and gently slip it into her hand, which is limp at first, then clamps down hard. She looks at the phone, looks at me, smiles and takes a deep breath, puts the phone in her pocket with someone still talking on the other end. She goes to the kitchen and quickly comes back with my lunch, two cheeseburgers with French fries and a Coke. My mouth starts watering, but I manage to say: This isn't what I ordered.

She says: Of course it's not what you ordered. It's what you wanted.

I say: But it's not on the menu.

She says: The cook is a burger addict. He keeps a private stash of ground beef in the freezer, and he's also got fries and Cokes. It's what he always has for lunch—in secret of course. This time I told him to make a few extra cheeseburgers. He's a good guy and he always tries to give people what they want. And so do I.

I say: How did you know what I wanted?

She says: I'm good at what I do.

I nod and smile and think about asking how she learned to read minds. But she pulls out her phone and starts talking again, picking up right where she left off before, squinting like someone who can't quite make out the words on a teleprompter. It sounds like she's getting pulled back into a painful situation, like she's just about to forget that she can't get along with the guy on the phone. I want to tap her shoulder and say *Don't forget*. But I've missed my chance. She's rushing back into the kitchen, telling him that just the sight of his number on her phone last night got her so worked up that she ran out to the convenience store and stuffed herself with Twinkies, then spent the rest of the night vomiting, trying to talk herself out of calling him back. There's no doubt that she's good at what she does, and maybe she's even got a Ph.D. in psycholinguistics, but when it comes to relationships of passion, it sounds like she's just as confused as everyone else.

The wind is banging hard against the window. It's so intense that it looks like it might start ripping trees out of the ground. Trash is spiraling into the sky, darkening the sun. Even the Museum of Man looks like it might be in danger. Earlier the wind felt like it was making my confusion worse. Now I want nothing more than to be outside and feel its power. I leave two twenty-dollar bills on the table, as if by paying for food I haven't consumed I could leave my hunger behind. It hurts to leave those juicy burgers uneaten. But even if I'm under a spell, it's good to know I can still refuse. I assume that if Craig were still here, he'd say that I've taken a radical action.

# STOPPING

At some point in your life, you reach a stopping point. You come to a place where the only thing you can do is stop and wait. You won't know why you've stopped. You won't have an explanation later. It's not something you can anticipate or prepare for. It just happens.

For Honey Stone, the stopping point was near the Brooklyn Bridge. She got up at half past two in the morning and went outside for a walk. The fog of lower Manhattan was thick. There might have been dangerous people walking the streets. But she knew she had to get out. Her apartment felt like the wrong place to be. It wasn't that the two women she lived with were being difficult. In fact they were pleasant people, and the place was large and well designed, so they didn't get in each other's way. And it wasn't that Honey Stone was in a tough situation. She had good friends, a steady job, and no boyfriend problems.

But she knew she was in the wrong place. She knew she had to be somewhere else. She walked down Broadway watching herself appear and disappear and reappear in the darkened shop fronts. The streetlights floated in the mist. Her footsteps told her where she was going. She walked into City Hall Park and saw the lights of the Brooklyn Bridge. She told herself to stop. She took a step, took another step, and stopped.

Silence moved in every direction at once. She had no words to give the moment shape. If a gust of wind suddenly ripped through the fog, blowing discarded pages of a *New York Times* across the pavement, it made no impression. She had no words to tell herself what she was looking at, no words to tell herself that she had no words to tell herself what she looking at, no words to explain why time was no longer trapped in the sound of her footsteps, no words for the lights of the Brooklyn Bridge, while more than fifty blocks uptown, thirty floors above the street, Harry Knight was looking out a window toward the Brooklyn Bridge, relaxing into the jazz and dim blue light of a late-night party, ignoring all the talk that filled the room. He wasn't there to socialize. He was there to please the host, a man who owned the music store where Harry Knight had a part-time job. Now that Harry Knight had made himself look happy and social, talking and laughing his way around the room, nodding at all the appropriate times, telling his boss what a great time he was having, he felt free to sit back and lose himself in the jazz and the Brooklyn Bridge. But a white-haired man in a black shirt pulled up a chair, meeting Harry Knight's eyes, putting a deck of cards on the table between them.

Harry Knight was annoyed. He didn't want to be bothered keeping up a conversation, especially not with someone he'd never seen before. But Harry Knight was polite. His mother had taught him not to hurt people's feelings, even if it meant that he had to set aside his own feelings. So he smiled at the white-haired man and the white-haired man smiled back. Then the white-haired man shuffled the deck and placed five cards face-down on the table.

He said: Choose a card and place it face-up on the table.

The card that Harry Knight picked was unfamiliar. Instead of an ace of spades or two of clubs, or one of the emblems in a tarot pack, the face of the card was an eye that opened and closed four times, then disappeared. Harry Knight briefly felt like four different people, each of whom briefly felt like four different people, each of whom briefly felt like four different people, each of whom briefly felt like four different people.

He lifted his eyes from the card and smiled at the man and the man smiled back and said: Care to pick another card?

The next card was a green ear nesting in blood-red notes of music. It made him think that music was in his blood, that his ear was always green, always new, when he heard great music. But the music on the card made him feel like dancing, and dancing made him feel self-conscious and awkward, while the music in the room was calm and expansive, like an easy chair with a view of an urban skyline. The ear on the card heard nothing, and the blood-red music made no sound, which made him feel that he must have lost his hearing, that the jazz and the talk of the party was all in his head.

The next card was a pile of teeth beside a glass of water. Harry Knight suddenly felt like eating and drinking. He was just about to get up and find food and beer, but the white-haired man smiled and asked him to pick another card. There were two cards left on the table. Harry Knight wondered if the choice made any difference, if the stakes of the game were higher than he thought. Perhaps he was choosing between right and wrong or life and death. But the white-haired man seemed harmless, so Harry Knight picked up another card, which showed a king-size bed with a nose instead of a pillow. Harry Knight put his hand on his nose, stroked it with his thumb, making sure it still felt like his own nose and not someone else's. Then he licked his teeth and put his hand on his mouth, as if to prevent words from getting out. But the gesture was unsuccessful, and Harry Knight heard himself telling the white-haired man to pick the last card himself. The man was blunt in his refusal, suddenly more serious than he seemed before. Harry Knight felt anxious, thought of changing the subject, then realized that he wasn't sure what the subject was, unless it was change itself, in which case changing the subject would be an example of the subject, and would only make his anxiety worse. He thought of getting up and leaving, but he knew it would be impolite not to take the last card.

He picked it up, expecting to find another facial feature. But the card was blank. Looking into its white rectangular space made Harry Knight dizzy. He closed his eyes. His mind was spinning in two directions at different speeds slowly becoming one speed. He opened his eyes. The table was empty. He looked around the room. It seemed to be looking back, then closing its eyes. The talk and the jazz were the same but the white-haired man with the black shirt wasn't there. Harry Knight looked again. He assumed that the man had gone to the bathroom. But when the bathroom door opened a few minutes later, a woman came out, bobbing her head to the music. Harry Knight scanned the room again. The white-haired man wasn't there, but this time his absence felt absolute, and a minute later even his absence wasn't there anymore, and the absence of the absence felt absolute. Harry Knight got up and left.

He walked out into the late-March fog with an unfamiliar feeling, as if he'd been stripped of his face, as if it hadn't been his to begin with. To someone else this might have been unpleasant. But Harry Knight accepted the feeling quickly, partly because he felt that his party face belonged at the party, that it had no business being anywhere else, and partly because the absence of his face was reassuring, briefly releasing him from a lifelong source of pain, the struggle to look at himself in the mirror, or to look at people looking at him passing on the street. It didn't occur to him that they might be more disturbed by the absence of his face than by its presence. But it did occur to him that in the dense fog no one was likely to get a good look at him. And it also occurred to him that most New Yorkers were so caught up in themselves that they rarely saw anyone else with clarity or interest.

Few things pleased Harry Knight more than foggy New York streets at three in the morning. He loved the silhouettes of pointed housetops, the dim reflections in dirty warehouse windows, the blurred imprint of streetlights on wet sidewalks, the sudden distorted shadows of people approaching or moving away. There were hundreds of ways of getting home, sequences of streets he could choose to follow, depending on what he wanted to see through the fog. He knew the streets by heart, by the sound of his footsteps on the pavement. He walked and came to corners under streetlights, turned and walked and came to other corners under streetlights, turned and walked and watched the streetlights floating in the mist, until he came to City Hall Park and the lights of the Brooklyn Bridge. He told himself to stop. He took a step, took another step, and stopped.

Silence filled his body like someone turning off a TV set. He had no words to give the moment shape, no words to make the next moment replace the moment he'd left behind, as if he could only be where he was by cooling down or heating up, slowing down or speeding up, as if the words *down* and *up* had created each other, negated each other, leaving him with no words to explain that he had no words to explain where he was, no words to explain why time was no longer trapped in the sound of his footsteps, no words for the lights of the Brooklyn Bridge, no words for the woman standing beside him, except that he knew she too had stopped.

Earlier that day, at precisely the same time, Honey Stone and Harry Knight had decided for the millionth time that President Bush was a pig. He was worse than a pig; he was a menace. He was worse than a menace; he was a mass murderer. He was worse than a mass murderer; he was a mass murderer disguised as a Christian hero. For nearly seven years he'd been a major disgrace to the nation, supported by and supporting a vast network of rich and dangerous people. Honey Stone and Harry Knight had decided that George Bush had to get what he deserved. He had to be arrested and tried as a war criminal and sent to the electric chair, a televised execution. And since they knew that this would never happen, they decided that someone had to assassinate him, and they hated themselves for lacking the guts to do it, which reminded them of all the other things they'd never had the guts to do, all the possibilities they'd missed out on because they'd been afraid.

The fact that they were the only people in the world who'd had exactly the same thought at exactly the same time and had later come to exactly the same place at exactly the same time broke the spell. They started again, in the midst of what sounded like an extended conversation.

He said: You're absolutely right. All jobs are stupid. I refuse to work full-time. I'd rather live on almost nothing than waste my time doing stupid things just because someone tells me to.

She said: It's not that I hate my job. As jobs go, it's not bad, and I like some of the people I work with. But it's like you said: I don't want to waste time doing what someone tells me to do—

He said: Especially when the things they tell you to do are things you wouldn't choose to do on your own.

She said: Or if I did choose to do them on my own, I'd do them the way I wanted to do them, at my own pace, in my own way, without having to deal with someone telling me when and how—

He said: For example, if you got up to sharpen a pencil, you'd look out the window and watch pigeons eating breadcrumbs on the sidewalk. And on your way back to your desk you'd play with yourself in the company bathroom. Before you started writing again, you'd—

She said: Or if I was typing an important memo, I'd make every other sentence openly or secretly ridiculous, and the person reading it would consciously or unconsciously know that nothing can be serious unless it's also funny. If I was—

He said: It's getting late.

She said: I think you're right.

They turned and started walking across the Brooklyn Bridge. The lights of lower Manhattan towered in fog behind them. A dark network of old industrial buildings waited in fog in front of them. They didn't say anything. Silence was better. Words would only have blocked out what they already knew, kept them from arriving at Harry Knight's tiny apartment, one room with a kitchenette and bathroom in Vinegar Hill, a neighborhood most New Yorkers had never been to, or even heard of, until the more popular neighborhoods became unaffordable.

She sat on his bed. He sat on the chair he pulled out from his desk.

She said: Nice little place you've got here. I wouldn't mind living here myself. The view of the harbor is great. And I love the hardwood floors. In my apartment everything is carpeted. It's really stupid.

He looked outside and saw lights moving in the harbor fog. He suddenly realized that the fog wasn't masking his face any longer. For a second he felt exposed. But when he studied Honey Stone's face he saw no alarm, and he assumed that either his eyes and nose and mouth were back in place, or that Honey Stone didn't think she knew him well enough to tell him to his face that he had no face.

He said: There's nothing better than a window filled with lights in harbor fog.

She said: How long have you had this place?

He looked at the old portrait framed above his desk, a man with white hair and a black shirt. It occurred to him for the first time in his life that he didn't know who the man was. He heard a car approaching three floors down. He heard it stop, doors opening and slamming shut, indistinct voices, footsteps on pavement, then silence, then a foghorn in the distance.

She said: How long have you had this place?

He got up and went to the bathroom, closing the door behind him. Honey Stone waited a long time without moving, watching the lights in the fog. Finally she propped up the pillows against the wall, leaned back and lit a cigarette, blowing smoke rings and watching them fade. She looked at the bathroom door, as if by staring hard enough she might make him reappear. But the door was flat and white as an empty page, and Honey Stone knew that the page would remain empty, simply because so many things that could have been written there hadn't been. She tucked herself under the covers, turned off the light, and closed her eyes. The foghorns made her sleep feel safe and relaxing.

When she woke the clock on the wall said half past nine. The fog was still thick. It took her a while to figure out that she wasn't in her own room, even though a portrait of her father was framed on the wall. She looked at the bathroom door and slowly remembered Harry Knight, how he'd gone to the bathroom and never come out. She figured he must have been drunk and passed out on the floor, even though he seemed sober the night before. But when she opened the door he wasn't there. She assumed he must have gotten up earlier and gone out, so she got back under the covers and waited.

The street was quiet. The fog was thick enough to swallow all the noise of the city, making her feel that the room was the only place in the world. Thoughts came slowly. Each word stretched out for fifteen minutes, losing its verbal form and becoming a fish. She spent the whole day underwater. The fog was getting dark. Soon she lay back down and went to sleep.

When she opened her eyes, the day was cool and bright and the street was full of sounds. She saw the lower Manhattan skyline through the window, the Manhattan Bridge, the Brooklyn Bridge, the towering space that had once been the World Trade Center. The clock said half past eight, and she was due at work by nine. She picked up Harry Knight's phone and called in sick. There was still no sign of him, but she was hungry, so she put on a pot of coffee, took bacon and eggs from his refrigerator and made herself a delicious breakfast. Then she went downstairs and wandered around the neighborhood. Honey Stone had never been to Vinegar Hill before, and she liked what she saw. Much of it was industrial, battered brick warehouses with broken windows, but the old residential buildings, cobbled streets, and sleepy cafés made it seem like 1900. She knew she would have liked it even more fifteen years ago, before the artists came and the place became chic, before the yuppies came and the place became unaffordable. But something about the neighborhood still felt immune to gentrification.

Honey Stone got a ham sandwich from a place with a sign that promised *Hot Meals!* but otherwise had no name. Then she went back to Harry Knight's apartment. He still wasn't there. She noticed that he'd left his wallet on the nightstand, and she decided to go through it and find out who he was. But aside from four one-dollar bills, the wallet was empty—no credit cards, no ID cards, no pictures of smiling relatives. She opened the drawer of an old wooden desk and examined his personal papers, which told her only one crucial fact, that Harry Knight wasn't paying rent on his apartment. Apparently, it had been in the family for decades. When his mother died in 1980, Harry Knight got a free apartment, except for the $50 a month he paid in property taxes.

She couldn't resist a strange but seductive thought: What if Harry Knight was gone? What if she could stay in his apartment, reducing her housing expenses to $50 a month? She lay down on Harry Knight's bed and did some delicious math. With the $25,000 she'd managed to save in the ten years she'd been working in the city, she could pay his taxes for ten years and still have almost $20,000 left over. If she lived carefully, she could get by without working!

She soon fell into a sleep that felt like falling asleep a thousand times, and when she woke up to another cool clear morning and Harry Knight wasn't there, she called her boss and quit her job, took one of the books on Harry Knight's desk and went to a small café on the corner, happier than she'd ever been in her life. Honey Stone took a table near the open doorway, looking down the street toward the docks and the river, paging through the book and reading passages here and there. The book was called *Eat Pork!*—a memoir about the death of the author's mother—but nothing that she read explained the title.

The waiter put a menu on the table. The prices were low by Manhattan standards, and though she knew on her limited budget she couldn't take many meals outside her apartment, for now she wanted to celebrate her new situation without fussing about money. The waiter must have been over seven feet tall. He was standing in the light coming in through the windows, eyebrows raised and pencil poised above the pad in his giant spider-like hand. She managed to say that she wanted eggs Benedict and coffee, but felt too overwhelmed by her new situation to say anything else, which was fine with the waiter, who as a rule had no interest in conversations since they made him feel awkward, as if he were suddenly in a room that was only large enough to contain his head. So he smiled at Honey Stone and turned toward the kitchen, took one step, took another step, and stopped.

Silence made the café seem like an answer on a final exam, as if he were solving a difficult calculus problem without writing anything down, doing it all in his head, not even using numbers, picturing the elements of the problem as a pattern of images: a cage in a research lab, a shack made of junk in a desert canyon, a half moon above mountains framed by a casement window, a classroom surrounded by teeth on burning billboards, a tower piercing a windy afternoon sky—images arranged and rearranged, mixing with and replacing each other, passing through each other, falling into place and falling out of place, as if the two motions were the same thing, as if all numbers were secretly other numbers, or became other numbers at high altitudes and low temperatures.

The silence reminded Honey Stone that she'd left her purse on Harry Knight's bed. She got up and left. But the waiter, Lance Boyle, stood there smiling, caught between seconds, eyes halfway between the words on his waiter's pad and the double doors of the kitchen. There was no way to know how long he stopped. Everything around him stayed exactly as it was. There was no one else waiting for breakfast, and the cook in the kitchen had gone to sleep. The moment was free to cast aside its temporal disguise. It was no longer simply a dot on a line, so now it began to expand above and beside and below that line, relaxing into unlimited space in every direction, except that now it could no longer be called a moment—it was taking too long for a moment—which meant that it was left without a name, without a way to hold itself in place, and it fell and smashed on the floor like a broken egg, forcing Lance Boyle to bend and clean it up, since he knew his boss would be there soon. His boss would go berserk if the floor was a mess.

He'd always hated bending to clean things up, not because he thought he was too good to clean up his own mess, but because bending always reminded him of how tall he was, how his height had always been a problem. Lance Boyle wasn't good at basketball and thought he looked like a jerk when he walked. This feeling had been with him since he was five, when he started getting taller than everyone else, and all the kids on the block began making fun of the way he walked. Things got even worse later, when the one girl he'd ever taken out on a date giggled and said that he looked like the mast of a ship in a storm when he walked. Though she'd apologized when he complained about how bad the analogy made him feel—she told him she didn't really mean it and was just trying to be clever, seeing if the simile worked well enough to include in a poem she was working on—he still never got over it. He never wanted anyone to see him walking again. He'd always felt better sitting down so no one could tell how tall he was. But he couldn't wait on tables sitting down, and it was the only job he could find, since studies had shown that extremely tall people made smaller people nervous. Few employers wanted people over seven feet tall working for them.

But something about the way Honey Stone had sized him up made Lance Boyle think that she might want to be his friend. So he went outside to see if he could find out where she'd gone. The street was empty, but there was a footprint on the sidewalk. When he went down on all fours to get a better look, he picked up a scent and told himself that it had to be Honey Stone's. Lance Boyle had a great nose, and he followed the scent down the street, walking quickly on all fours, around a corner and down another street, sniffing carefully, wagging his tail, around a corner and down another street, sniffing his way through patches of light and shade on the filthy sidewalk, around the corner and down another street, sniffing and wagging his tail, until a woman jogging in a black sweatsuit caught up with him, scratched behind his ears, kissed the top of his head, circled his neck with a collar, hooked a leash to the collar, and took him down the block, unlocked a steel door, took him up three flights of stairs to a small apartment with a view of the Brooklyn Bridge. He circled three times on the sky-blue oval carpet, settled down and looked up at his master, who scratched behind his ears again. Then she got up and went to the bathroom, threw off her sweats, and took a shower.

She'd never loved anything more than taking showers. In fact, she jogged every day in winter and early spring not because keeping in shape was crucial, but because she liked getting sweaty on cold mornings and having to take long showers, warming the grime and exhaustion out of her body. Dawn Wakeman worked in the towel section of a department store in downtown Brooklyn. She liked the work because towels reminded her of taking showers, and she thought constantly of all the showers her customers would be taking. No two showers were alike. The sounds and caressing motions of the water, the interplay of light and steam, the scented soaps and shampoos and conditioners, the patterns of relaxation unfolding in every part of her body—all of them happened in different ways each time she took a shower. Dawn Wakeman was convinced that if people could learn to appreciate all the differences in the showers they took day after day, boredom would become a thing of the past. She'd even thought of offering classes in the art of taking showers, but she had cancelled the idea when she realized that formalizing the process into a sequence of lessons would destroy the pleasure that played such a strong part in her life each day.

Besides, she knew that guys would sign up for the class for the sole purpose of taking showers with women, and Dawn Wakeman couldn't imagine showering with anyone else. She'd never understood why people thought it was sexy to shower with lovers. A friend once told her that if you weren't happy showering with a guy, you better find someone else. But lovers had become a thing of the past for Dawn Wakeman. Men had always been too selfish and mean, and she no longer thought about going to bed with a woman. She much preferred the company of Lance, her five-year-old Great Dane. He was never anything but affectionate, and she loved the way that he slept at the foot of her bed. She'd even gotten a larger bed to make room for him when he grew from being a sweet little puppy into a sweet enormous adult. Though sometimes he got lost and wandered around the neighborhood, his large size made him easy to find, especially when everyone in Vinegar Hill knew whose dog he was and would quickly return him if they found him alone on the street.

Dawn Wakeman often wondered if there wasn't something weird about her preference for a dog. But five years back, right before she adopted Lance from the dog pound, she had an experience that clarified everything. She'd been taking a vacation in southern

Oregon, walking the cliffs and enjoying the cold gray skies, taking three showers each day in the inexpensive room she'd found five miles outside a town that no one had ever heard of. Everything was desolate and deserted, until one day she saw someone sitting on a rock at the foot of the cliffs, carefully watching the sea and making sketches in a large black book. At first she had no reaction. But as the days passed and she kept seeing the man sitting one hundred feet below making sketches in his book, she became curious. Finally she descended. She found a rugged pathway winding down the side of the cliff. It wasn't entirely safe, but she took the risk anyway, telling herself to be careful. Measuring every step, she finally got to the bottom, only to find that the man was no longer there.

Day after day, the same thing happened. She saw the man sketching and carefully made her way down the cliff, finding herself alone when she got to the bottom. She saw no other way up the cliff, saw no caves that the man might have been hiding in, and from above had seen no boat that he might have used as a means of escape. She tried to keep her eyes on the man while climbing down the path, but this was impossible, since the way was slippery and difficult. If she'd lifted her eyes at any point, she might have fallen to her death. Whenever she stopped and steadied herself to look down he was still there sketching. But whenever she got to the foot of the cliff he was gone, as if he existed only when seen from above.

She would have given up if something hadn't been wrong with the sea. She couldn't say what it was at first, except that the light on the water looked fake. Then she became convinced that the man was responsible, that he'd been taking the waves and sketching them into his notebook, appropriating the ocean with pencil and page. She knew the thought was insane, and the more she let it circulate the more insane it became. She had to make it stop. But each day the ocean was smaller, two percent smaller, five percent smaller, shrinking and sinking, wrinkling up like shriveled skin or a yellowing page, fading away from the sound it normally made when it crashed on the shore.

She knew there was only one thing to do. Stuffing a knapsack with food and blankets, she found a hiding place behind rocks at the foot of the cliff, waiting for the man to show up with his sketchbook. Day after day, the result was the same: He never came, and the ocean stopped getting smaller. Even the missing waves came back to crash on the rocks and return to the sea. She never saw the man again. She went back to her daily walks on the cliff and felt proud of herself. Her showers were even more beautiful than before. She flew back to Vinegar Hill convinced that she'd saved the Pacific Ocean.

She told her girlfriends that men were a thing of the past. When they asked why, she shrugged and said that men were too destructive. The result was a burst of agreement. Her friends agreed that men were too destructive, but they also agreed that this was nothing new, and they also agreed that men were convinced that women were too destructive, which meant that nothing would change, that they couldn't imagine themselves without men, and so they agreed with each other that Dawn Wakeman would soon be dating again, that she wasn't meant to spend her life by herself. She agreed that she wasn't meant to spend the rest of her life by herself. But she saw no reason to settle for human companionship.

At first, the absence of men was strange. When she'd sworn them off in the past, she'd always imagined herself with women. But now she wasn't imagining much of anything. Instead, she was stepping out of one of the ten most relaxing showers she'd ever taken, drying herself off with one of her many towels, laughing at the very thought of forcing herself again to accept the confusions and frustrations of an intimate human relationship. In fact, she'd even tried to write an essay for *Ms. Magazine* denouncing the process of couple formation. But writing always made her insecure, and besides, she'd already saved the Pacific Ocean from the human race. She didn't also need to save the human race from itself.

She was just about to scratch Lance behind his ears and run a brush through her long black hair when the sight of the Brooklyn Bridge out the window made her pause. It often made her pause. But this was different. Something about the light on the river made food seem tempting. Something about the light on the river made food seem disgusting. The two feelings couldn't exist at the same time, so both disappeared. She took a step, another step, and stopped.

Silence filled the room like every sky she'd ever seen. She felt like the Brooklyn Bridge at five in the morning. She felt like she'd spent the last five years of her life with Friends of Silence, an underground society of mental ecologists who spent their free time eliminating media noise, cleverly and politely convincing the owners of bars, restaurants, pharmacies, laundromats, and supermarkets to remove all radios and TVs from their places of business, liberating huge expanses of mental space from commercial interference, an event of even greater importance than the removal of cigarette smoke from public places. Her entire life seemed to be an ongoing series of interventions in the name of silence, and the thought that she could continue this work for the rest of her life was beautiful enough to make her take a step, and another step, leashing her dog and going downstairs to the street, eagerly searching out her next intervention.

She found one quickly. A few blocks away, through the window of a small café, she could see a TV above the bar, the face of President Bush, then a beer commercial. Dawn Wakeman tied her dog by the leash to a parking meter, went inside, and asked to speak to the owner. As it turned out, he was tending bar.

Dawn Wakeman said: Can you turn the TV off?

The owner smiled: I could, but I don't think I will.

Dawn Wakeman said: Why not?

The owner's smile disappeared: Why should I turn it off?

Dawn Wakeman said: It's making noise. It's bullshit.

The owner said: My customers don't think so.

Dawn Wakeman said: Why don't we ask them?

He said: Studies have shown that people like eating in places where stupid music plays in the background. I assume that my customers are the same as the people in the studies.

Dawn Wakeman said: Fuck the studies! Why don't we ask them?

Dawn Wakeman turned and looked at the people drinking coffee at the tables. She said: How many of you would be upset if we turned the TV off?

No one said anything.

Dawn Wakeman turned back to the owner and said: So turn the TV off.

He shrugged and turned the TV off.

Dawn Wakeman said: Thanks. Can I use your bathroom?

He pointed to a door by the kitchen. Dawn Wakeman went to the bathroom and looked at herself in the mirror. Leaning over the sink, she moved her face close to the glass and inspected her teeth. They were perfectly straight and white. She'd always been convinced that her teeth were the part of her face that men liked best, but ever since she'd given up on men, she thought of her teeth not as instruments of glamour and seduction, but as things to bite with. When she wasn't focused on showers and towels, she thought about what she could bite, and though she'd never actually bitten anyone, whenever she saw politicians on TV or in the papers, her teeth felt sharper, and her mouth was filled with predatory cravings.

The impulse made her feel foolish and guilty. After all, it wasn't ladylike, and her parents had brought her up to behave in a dignified manner, even around people who didn't deserve it. The nation's current leaders didn't deserve it. But now that she'd replaced the President's televised face with silence, she felt less violent, calm enough to pull her teeth away from the mirror and go back out and have cake and coffee, luxuriating in the media-free atmosphere she'd created. She took a table near the doorway, glancing out the window down the cobbled street to the river. A young man over seven feet tall approached and took her order.

Dawn Wakeman said: Isn't it much nicer now that we don't have listen to the President's lies and a bunch of advertising jingles?

Lance Boyle looked over his shoulder to make sure his boss wasn't listening, then softly said: Absolutely.

Dawn Wakeman liked the way Lance Boyle said *absolutely*. There was something about the look in his eyes that made her think of her dog. She thought she better quickly check to see how her dog was doing, but when she stepped outside she didn't see him. She leaned back in through the doorway and told Lance Boyle: Looks like my dog got away. I better go find him.

Lance Boyle: I wish I could come and help you look. But things are pretty busy here right now.

Dawn Wakeman smiled and said: Oh that's okay. I'll find him.

She turned and walked away quickly.

Lance Boyle was amazed. He couldn't believe that the TV had been turned off. His boss was the kind of guy who never compromised about anything, even when he was clearly wrong. Yet Dawn Wakeman had gotten what she wanted, like someone with a knack for making dogs obey commands, though apparently her own dog wasn't always obedient. He hoped that Dawn Wakeman's dog was large, a Saint Bernard or Great Dane, because a large dog would be much easier to find than a small dog, which could easily disappear behind garbage cans or between buildings.

A woman came in and sat in Dawn Wakeman's empty seat. She looked so much like Dawn Wakeman that at first Lance Boyle thought they were twins. But when he came to her table and gave her a menu, he saw that she didn't look anything like Dawn Wakeman. The two impressions merged, two faces that looked the same and different at the same time, as if the same would never be the same again, as if difference made no difference, as if the words that kept telling him a story about himself, changing the subject over and over again until everything sounded the same, had reached a point where the subject made no difference, and the story would never be told the same way again. Lance Boyle took a step back, took another step back, and stopped.

Silence pooled itself on people's plates, becoming the greatest meal they'd ever tasted. They stuffed themselves and would have called for more, but they didn't need to speak to place their orders. The silence pooled itself on their plates automatically, and each new dish was even more delicious than the one before. The silence also made the lighting softer, made everyone look their best, and Lance Boyle savored himself in the mirror, fell in love with his height, felt relaxed and confident when he the took the woman's order.

Honey Stone was puzzled when she met the waiter's eyes. When she'd seen him in the café before, she could tell he felt strange about his height. But something about him had changed, and when she told him what she wanted she could see how pleased he was that she was looking at him. Over the years, Honey Stone had learned to read in people's faces what they thought of themselves, not what they told themselves about themselves, but what their cells felt about sharing a shape with each other, contributing to the same organic system. She'd gotten so perceptive that she'd considered marketing her methods, offering classes in the art of reading people's bodies.

But a few nights before, she'd met a man she couldn't read. She'd drawn such a blank from the message of his body that she'd lost it completely. She knew he was somewhere in his own bathroom, but she couldn't find him, and she'd gotten so confused that she'd actually concluded that she could start living in his apartment, paying almost nothing for a space with a lovely view of New York Harbor. Now that she saw the change in the waiter's body, she knew what to look for in the man she'd lost track of, and she got up and left without waiting for the waiter, dashing down the street, outrunning the sound of her footsteps back to the room she'd begun to call home.

Honey Stone looked out the window into the gathering fog. Her body began to relax as the night came on. The motion of the lights in the harbor pulled her slowly into a trance, releasing all the words in her head from their customary shapes and sounds. She turned and met the face of Harry Knight coming out of the bathroom.

He said: It's getting late.

She said: I think you're right.

They left and walked in silence through the maze of industrial streets, across the Brooklyn Bridge to the lights in the fog of City Hall Park. When they came to a bench, they told themselves to stop. They looked at each other. No footsteps approached or moved away. No garbage was blown by wind across the pavement. There were streetlamps near the benches in the park and lights in the harbor fog. But no one coughed or laughed or lit a cigarette in the distance. No sirens made the night seem filled with tragedy and menace. No cabs or trucks went by, and no one screamed or wept or tripped and fell. But Harry Knight and Honey Stone were surprised when they looked at each other, as if they weren't expecting what they saw. They took a step back from each other, took another step back from each other, and stopped.

They both had a lot to think about. But they weren't thinking. It's true that if you saw them standing there in the fog, looking like they were just about to say or do something else, you'd probably assume that they were thinking, that the silence was filled with unspoken words, possibly important words. But when you reach the stopping point, you don't think. Everything just happens. The noise that's been in your head all your life isn't there. It's like it never was.

**STEPHEN-PAUL MARTIN**, former editor of *Central Park* magazine, has published many books of fiction, non-fiction, and poetry. He is currently a Professor of English at San Diego State University.